UNDERCOVER . . .
ON ENEMY GROUND!

Around four o'clock on the afternoon of Sunday, December 10, a nondescript young woman approached Vera Nevsky at the foot of the statue of Yuri the Long Arm and asked her to come for a walk.

When they had walked down as far as Nikita Gates, a man came up to them, spoke a few quiet words to Vera's walking companion, and then handed the package containing the documents over to Vera Nevsky . . . *As if it were a bomb, and might go off any moment!*

If a KGB agent had been nearby, he would have become immediately suspicious . . .

Bantam Books by Harry Arvay
Ask your bookseller for the books you have missed

ELEVEN BULLETS FOR MOHAMMED
THE MOSCOW INTERCEPT
OPERATION KUWAIT
THE PIRAEUS PLOT

The Moscow Intercept

Harry Arvay

THE MOSCOW INTERCEPT

A Bantam Book / November 1975

Published simultaneously in the United States and Canada

Bantam Books are published by Bantam Books, Inc. Its trademark, consisting of the words "Bantam Books" and the portrayal of a bantam, is registered in the United States Patent Office and in other countries. Marca Registrada. Bantam Books, Inc., 666 Fifth Avenue, New York, New York 10019.

PRINTED IN THE UNITED STATES OF AMERICA

The Main Protagonists

The Russians

DR. ILIYA PETROVITCH NEVSKY—Professor of Bacteriology and Epidemiology, Moscow State University

VERA NEVSKY—His wife

DR. IGOR ALEXANDREVITCH STANIEV—Professor of Pharmacology, University of Leipzig

DR. YURI SLONIN—Former Professor of Epidemiology, Moscow State University; new immigrant to Israel, attached to the "Section for Unconventional Weapons" of Israel's Security Branch (SB)

The Israelis

MAX ROTH—Head of the Counter-Terror Department, SB European Section

COLONEL DAVID BORAN—Chief of European Section, Military Intelligence, attached to Roth's office

ITZHAK—Alias Heinrich Schuehler, alias Samuel Meiersohn. Member of the SB Commando Unit

HEIDI—His wife, alias Ilse Schuehler, Alias Paula Ginsberg. Member of the special SB Commando Unit

BARUCH—Alias Fritz Hansel, alias Misha Lipsky. Member of the special SB Commando Unit

99—Head of the Israeli underground cell in Moscow

Author's Note

This episode in the adventures of the Special Security Branch Commando Unit, continues to deal with highly topical contemporary affairs. The actions herein described touch upon the lives of people as well as existing organizations, institutions, and installations. I have used means available to the writer of fiction to protect these who must not be endangered.

Moscow is an enormous city.

The number of important thoroughfares and public squares far exceeds those in London, though the population is approximately half. A story of this nature taking place in Oxford Street, Regent Street, Picadilly Circus, or Trafalger Square would allow the author to keep location names to a minimum. This is not true of Moscow.

I do hope the fascination of such an unusual city justifies the effort the reader is called upon to familiarize himself with names having as many as fourteen letters. Similarly, I hope the names of my protaganists and their aliases will not pose any difficult problems.

The plot described is anything but farfetched. Black September is known to have at its disposal sophisticated weapons of Soviet origin such as portable antiaircraft missiles. The possibility of having poison gas or other materials of germ warfare put indiscriminately into their hands is well within the bounds of stark reality.

Nevertheless, I must stress that the specific places, circumstances, and dates described in my narrative are all fictitious.

—Harry Arvay

. . . 1

Leah Blum was at her wit's end. That morning, her boss, ordinarily the most considerate of men, had not only stacked work on her desk that would take her a week to do—if she hurried. He had also snarled at her.

It was, she knew, the state of his business that caused both the work overload and the snarl. An architect, her boss had only yesterday lost a contract for a housing development—into which he had put months of work—to his chief rival, a big architectural firm.

It had been a blow to his pride and his bank account, and Leah couldn't blame him. But it didn't stop her from flinching, either. She had done more than flinch. She had begun to tremble and now, ten minutes later, she was still trembling. She hadn't been able to stop.

The telephone rang. Leah picked up the receiver. She was on the verge of tears (something she detested more in women than men) when she said "Hello," her voice quavering.

"Leah Blum, please."

"This is she."

"Good morning. This is Tony Rankin."

Tony Rankin! She had been waiting two weeks—praying—for his call.

"Hello . . ." she said again, her voice still quavering as she fought to control her feelings.

"I was wondering," said Tony, "well, I thought you might be free for dinner tonight. I know it's late to call."

Free for dinner! Leah tried not to make her "Yes, I

am. Yes," too blatantly eager. Tony Rankin was a reporter. He got to Jerusalem, he had told Leah when she'd met him two weeks ago at a party, every month or so, and could he call her?

"Terrific," he answered. "Shall I pick you up?"

"Yes, Tony, why don't you," she managed to say, her voice almost normal, and she even managed to give him her correct address.

He was the most exciting unattached man she had ever met.

How could she get through the rest of the day? How could she work through such excitement?

She had her lunch sent in. Just soup. Lentil soup from the delicatessen downstairs. That would save her half an hour.

It was delicious.

She couldn't have eaten anything solid, not thinking about her first date with Tony Rankin. The soup was just right.

Cool. She had to be cool.

She began to type a boring letter to a London engineering school about the effects of Israel's climate on various building materials.

Suddenly she felt nauseous. She began to vomit before she collapsed in her chair. Twenty minutes later, she was discovered by her boss and rushed to a hospital.

Five blocks away, Alex Feldman was walking slowly in the midday heat when he decided to sit down on a bench and rest.

At forty-two, his skin was permanently sunburned to the color of dark brown wood. His coloring—his flashing blue eyes and prematurely gray hair—and the sharply defined lines of his face gave him the look of an actor, and people on the street often stared as he approached, stared as he passed, and stared as he continued on his way.

He must be *somebody!* Alex was used to this, though not at all disappointed if it didn't happen. He wasn't vain. And he wasn't *somebody.*

He was a florist. Actually he liked to think of himself as a gardener, for he grew his own flowers on his own land. But he spent most of his time inside his shop. Unloading flowers, arranging them, selling them.

Rested, his skin still dry in spite of the intense rays of the sun—he didn't sweat—Alex got up to resume his walk.

As he rose, his cane fell. He stooped to pick it up, feeling in advance the flash of pain he had learned to anticipate before certain movements. He had had a slight limp—enough to require a cane—since the Six Day War.

He crossed the street to the cafe on the other side, took a seat, and ordered tea. He sipped it quickly, for there was much to do when he got back to his shop.

Once more on the street, Alex was overcome by a dizziness he at first thought was caused by the sun. A violent attack of diarrhea followed before he fell flat onto the sidewalk.

Passersby gathered. One of them was a young intern, who had only to give him a superficial examination before pronouncing him dead.

Five floors above the cafe, it was 1:45 before Edith Schneider got the formula prepared.

She was baby-sitting for her daughter-in-law, Rose. Rose had gone shopping with a friend—her first time out of the apartment since bringing the baby, their firstborn, home from the hospital.

For Edith, it was a dream come true. Her first grandchild a boy! They had named him Benjamin after Edith's husband, who had died the year before.

A boy. Smiling, humming to herself, Edith took the baby tenderly in her arms and put the bottle to his mouth. The baby was hungry.

Edith sang a little lullaby. She had always had a good voice. She kept her eyes on Benjamin until he had finished, singing all the while. She barely had time to burp him before his little body went into convulsions.

Her face went white. She rushed to the telephone.

Evening newscasters in Jerusalem spoke of a sudden, mysterious outbreak of cholera. Hospital wards were jammed. Doctors were puzzled.

A new strain, they had labeled it, temporarily, *Vibrio cholerae 173*. No one knew its origin, though certain Israelis were already making very educated guesses.

Specialists from all over Israel were on their way to Jerusalem to isolate the germ, to stop it from spreading, to destroy it, if possible. In the meantime, all residents were told to boil their water thoroughly.

. . . 2

In Tel-Aviv, Max Roth's impromptu decision to call in Dr. Yuri Slonin had to be combined with the waiving of the normal rules of security screening procedures.

As a fairly recent immigrant from Russia, Slonin's dossier was less detailed and complete than that of an Israeli citizen of similar importance and background, but his dossier contained one item of information that outweighed any others. Yuri Slonin had been a fellow student of Iliya Petrovitch Nevsky, one of Russia's top researchers attached to the Soviet military laboratory concerned with germ warfare: the USSR Germinal War Defense Systems. The two scientists had remained close friends, despite political differences, and Slonin's immigration to Israel had been greatly expedited by Nevsky's help. Dr. Slonin seemed relaxed and quite at home at Security Branch Headquarters—as if he had spent years in these secretive, paramilitary surroundings.

"Have you had time to read the reports?" asked Roth. They had determined that only one well had been infected. After the second day, there were no significant further cholera attacks in Jerusalem or elsewhere in Israel.

So far . . .

"Yes it's very clear. I doubt that I can add much."

"Come, come, Doctor," said David Boran "You're too modest. It's not sufficient for us to know whether we're dealing with enemy sabotage or not. We need your expert opinion about the methods they employ in producing, preserving, and storing this germinal material."

Boran took out his pipe and began fussing with it. "We want to know how and by whom it has been produced; how it's transportable; how it can be most easily and safely destroyed. We want to know what quantities have to be used per cubic meter of water; how long the viscous matter that holds the germs in suspension takes to dissolve and mingle with the water; what kind of knowhow is required by the men who do the actual on-the-spot job of polluting our water system."

His pipe packed now, he put away his pouch, clenched the pipe between his teeth, and struck a match. He lit the pipe slowly, and talked between puffs. "In short, we have to know everything before we can be in a position to deal with this problem, before we have an epidemic on our hands."

Yuri Slonin seemed entirely at ease. "I would suggest, gentlemen, that we divide our problem into two separate parts. Naturally, they're connected even interrelated, but we'll have to approach them differently as far as timing, planning, method, and thinking are concerned."

Yuri Slonin's gaunt features seemed to shut out all distraction for a minute. He continued. "There's the local Jerusalem problem of prevention and cure, purifying the affected supply and guarding the unaffected water sources. There's also the problem of seeking out and apprehending the saboteurs and their collaborators."

He paused. "I think the local Jerusalem problems are being adequately taken care of by their health authorities. "Fortunately, comparatively little damage has been done so far. So little, in fact, that I suspect we are dealing only with a small-scale pilot project. The quantity and quality of this pollution attempt has been too localized to be termed anything more than experimental."

Max Roth and David Boran nodded thoughtfully.

"No, gentlemen," said Slonin, "it is quite clear to me that we are either dealing with a miniature operation, deadly though it's been, or we have only seen a small tryout. The latter seems more logical, when we consider how expertly the polluted material has been prepared, preserved, and transported." He paused and smiled. "Besides, you mentioned Iliya Nevsky."

"Yes." Roth replied. "Iliya Nevsky. Our Moscow operators have managed to obtain some fairly reliable information at the Mokhavaya Street Institute."

Slonin leaned forward in his chair and butted his cigarette in the ashtray on Roth's desk. "You mean the USSR Germinal War Defense System attached to the Old Moscow University Building?" Slonin asked rhetorically. "Of course, the cellars have been greatly extended to house the Institute, and my old friend Professor Nevsky has been working there for at least five years."

Roth leaned forward. "According to your knowledge then, how does the germ-warfare research carried out at Mokhavaya Street match what's been happening in Jerusalem?"

Yuri Slonin leaned back in his chair and smoked. He looked at the ceiling. He seemed to be hesitating. Then he said, "Hard to be certain. It's good work, and it would be typical of Nevsky to insist on having it tried out, at least under laboratory conditions, before using it in earnest."

"What do you mean by 'in earnest,' Doctor?" asked Boran.

"Well, from Nevsky's viewpoint, I doubt if it would include an Arab attack on Israel. He is more likely than not convinced that his present work thoroughly concerns the internal security of the Soviet Union. His nonscientific political superiors, however—those who direct the Institute—are very likely pleased about this rare opportunity: to try their germ-warfare potential in a real-life project on human guinea pigs.

Slonin made a face.

"In the old Stalin-Khrushchev days," he continued, "they would have used deportees in Siberia, or prisoners in the Urals. Now, they use the easy enemy. You can guess who that is."

Roth banged his hands on his desk and said emphatically, "Us!"

"Yes, gentlemen. I would suggest the distinct possibility of Moscow being Al Fatah's germ-warfare production center. Now we need to find the points of production and supply, and the people directly involved in Moscow and along the lines of transport and communication."

Deep silence settled over the room.

Then David Boran hammered the fist of his right hand into the palm of his left and said, "There's only one sure way to find out. We'll simply have to get inside the Mokhavaya Street Institute and look around."

Roth said, "Absolutely, Dave. All that remains to be done is to decide who goes to Moscow, and how soon."

Roth looked first at Boran, then at Slonin. "Baruch is my first choice. His parents are Russian, and he grew up in a Russian-speaking household. Also, his outward appearance is suitable. You'll be able to see for yourself, Doctor. He's blond, blue-eyed, rather heavily athletic, and he looks considerably older than twenty-seven or twenty-eight. He has enough education and experience as an overseas agent to pass himself off, in one capacity or another, inside a scientific institute."

Slonin said, "Yes . . . He sounds adequate. Of course, he wouldn't be able to achieve much alone. The setup in Moscow, and especially on Mokhavaya Street, is too complex to be handled by a solitary agent."

"That's only natural," Roth said. "He shall have company." He paused thoughtfully, and suddenly his round face became suffused with a grin. "Very congenial company, I might say."

Boran had observed Roth's metamorphosis from stern reflection to prankish humor, and he knew that his friend was waiting to be asked the meaning of his smile. "By congenial, I assume you mean a girl."

"Exactly, Dave. Who else but Heidi?"

Heidi was a beautiful German volunteer who had joined SB some years earlier and, among other operations, worked with SB's most successful commando unit in Germany and Scandinavia during the chase after the Black September commander, Mohammed. Heidi had married the leader of the SB group in question, and both she and her husband, Itzhak, had asked to be allowed to continue their work for Security Branch.

Boran objected. "Listen, Max. Itzhak doesn't know Russian, and neither does Heidi."

Slonin said, "Ah."

Roth rubbed his face with both hands, then put them down flat on the desk. "I'm aware of that." Then, turning to Slonin, he continued. "But first we should explain to Dr. Slonin who we're talking about."

Max Roth briefly outlined the background and character of the Israel-born Itzhak and his young German wife, bestowing upon them the highest praises for their efficient work as members of SB's most active commando unit.

"The other members of the group are Baruch, whom we've already mentioned, and two other fine men, Luke and Dov. There was another, Michael, but he's dead now."

Roth stared at his desk for a moment, then looked up. "Heidi and Itzhak don't speak Russian, but their German is perfect. I suggest we issue them with a set of East German documents that will pass the most painstaking inspection." He turned to Slonin. "What's your opinion, Doctor? In what capacity would it serve our purpose best to send these three to Moscow?"

Slonin took out a small pocket calendar and consulted a list of dates. "On the ninth of December, two weeks from today, there's a scientific convention at Moscow State University, to which scientists, chemists, physicians, and authorities from many fields have been invited." He flapped the calendar against his knee. "Security is bound to be more lax during such an event, and hundreds, maybe thousands, of strange faces in Moscow are certainly the best possible background for our operation." He paused. "Does Baruch know German?"

"Yes," said Boran "his German's excellent."

"Then they could both pass for East German scientists of one kind or another—Baruch and Itzhak, I mean. Heidi could simply be accompanying her husband. That's quite natural. Itzhak should have a membership card showing he belongs to the East German Communist Party. That will give him certain openings in Moscow which may prove advantageous. It'll also enhance the position of his wife."

Roth burst out laughing. Then his face sobered. "Fine, Doctor. I see you have the makings of a good SB agent. It shows that a scientific brain can function effectively outside the strict confines of its own field."

Slonin smiled. "Thank you for the compliment," he said. "It encourages me to make an additional suggestion. Baruch should keep his knowledge of Russian to himself. He might thus overhear things that will be helpful."

Boran nodded. "Good. Three guests from East Germany attending a scientific convention. What do you think their first step in Moscow should be, Doctor?"

"To visit Nevsky at home," Slonin said, without hesitation.

"How in hell can they do *that?*" Roth asked.

For the second time, Dr. Slonin smiled, but it was broader, and he interlaced his slender fingers in a prayer-like gesture.

"Heaven forbid that I should presume to teach members of Israel's renowned Security Branch how to do their jobs." He shook his head. "Still, music might be a useful gambit."

"Music?" Boran and Roth asked simultaneously.

"Yes. My friend Nevsky is a great music lover. Just mention music and he'll drag you to his house to listen to records. Vera likes music too, as I recall."

"Music is safe enough to begin with," said Boran. "How long does the convention last?"

"Five days, officially," Slonin said. "Though visitors from abroad will be arriving days before and staying longer, to see the sights of Moscow."

Roth leaned back in his chair. "Heidi, Itzhak, and Baruch are not going to be bored in Moscow."

"No doubt," said Boran. "Let's make sure they get back to tell the story!"

. . . 3

Heidi and Itzhak were delighted to hear about their forthcoming Moscow expedition. They received the urgent summons to Roth's office early on the morning of November 28 while they were still lying blissfully relaxed in each other's arms just after their usual morning lovemaking. Itzhak was caressing Heidi's lovely thighs, and kissing her breasts. They were both nude.

"We're two Security Branch agents on a short vacation, and we mustn't forget it," Itzhak said. He was joking.

Heidi had pulled his drooping blond mustache as he held his head a few inches above her face. Her own blue eyes laughingly challenged the loving look in his. His thick blond hair tumbled about his head.

Heidi asked, "Does that mean we'll go on copulating an average of three times a day—until the call of duty forces us to stop?"

"Your terminology is disgusting. Rabbits copulate. We make love. Otherwise, yes. The call of duty, as you well know, might separate us for weeks or even months, so we'd better make the best use of our time while we've got it." Itzhak laughed down at her.

"Agreed. Only let's not kill ourselves. Even we must eat sometime." Heidi jumped out of bed. Her dextrous judo twist dislodged Itzhak and spilled him on the thick carpet. "Breakfast coming up!"

"Goddamn you, Heidi!" His gaze seemed to eat at the smooth form of the lovely German girl.

"Now *you're* using bad words," she said.

"I'm your husband. You have to obey me."

"Like hell I do." She put her foot against his chest, and shoved him down to the carpet again.

But Itzhak was ready for her. He grabbed her ankle, and tripped her. She fell sprawling across him, and in another moment their lovemaking was in progress again.

"The hell with breakfast," Itzhak said.

But they were interrupted by the telephone. It was Max Roth. They were to go at once to his office.

They found Baruch already there, looking as dapper as ever.

"How's married life?" he asked.

"Not bad," Heidi said. "Why don't you try it?"

"Find me the right girl, Heidi. That's all I need."

They reminisced for a few minutes.

"Hello!" It was, Max Roth himself, smiling at them from the doorway.

"We were discussing our photographs on file with the police in various countrys." Itzhak's tone was sardonic.

"I suppose you could call those pinup of a sort," Roth commented as he slowly sat down behind his desk. "Dave will be joining us shortly, but let me give you the essentials now. To begin with, your holiday's over. It's back to work for the three of you."

"What about Luke and Dov?" Itzhak asked.

Roth said, "For the moment, it's just you three. You'll have to do a few days of intensive study and training before we give you your new ID's, and send you abroad."

Max Roth, catching looks of impatience that passed between Heidi and Itzhak, raised his hand like a traffic cop. "Stop! You'll be told all you have to know within five minutes. Ah, here comes Dave. Now we can begin in earnest."

Colonel David Boran looked as trim, neat, and athletic as ever. After they all had exchanged friendly greetings, Max Roth proceeded to give his listeners a detailed account of the events that had led up to the present meeting in his office. Concluding, he said, "They've made important strides in perfecting their methods of producing, storing, and transporting the *Vibrio cholerae* germs. They now have a viscous fluid that releases the live bacilli at a slow but deadly rate. 'Bacilli armoured,' as Slonin put it—is in a shell that withstands chlorination, and is finally dissolved only by the stomach juices."

Roth told them about Yuri Slonin's non-Jewish Russian friend, Professor Iliya Petrovitch Nevsky, now a senior scientist—possibly even a director—at the Moscow Germ Warfare Laboratory, situated in the cellars of the Old University on Mokhavaya Street.

He also gave them all the latest information he'd received on Abu Iyad, the leader of Black September, and Dr. George Habbash, head of the Palestine Liberation Front, both dedicated to the annihilation of Israel.

Namely, that containers filled with quantities of the new cholera pollutant, which was large enough to poison Israel's entire drinking-water system, were soon to be shipped to an undefined destination in one of the neighboring Arab states—Beirut, Bagdad, or Damascus. These containers would probably arrive direct from Russia on one of the regular Soviet airline flights.

Roth folded his hands on his desk. "Now comes the hard part. It's your job to find Nevsky. Then, if necessary, you're to get inside their labs and, somehow, find out when, how, and where this shipment is going to take place. If you can, of course, destroy it on the spot. But I see almost no chance for that. Otherwise, let us have exact details about their transportation operation. And the earlier, the better." Roth's owl-like eyes, behind his heavy bifocals, looked from one to the other. He was not smiling.

After a short silence, Baruch said, "How the hell do we get in? Who *are* we? Why should a leading scientist like Nevsky, working on a secret project, be willing to talk to us without calling in the KGB first?"

Boran explained the outline of their plan. Heidi interrupted him only once, when Slonin mentioned Mrs. Nevsky's interest in German fashions.

Heidi said, "I'll have to be brought up to date myself. It's been months since I read my last fashion magazine."

"Buy yourself a dozen," Roth said.

"When do we leave?" asked Itzhak.

Roth brought his fingers together into a pyramid. "I want you to have a few thorough sessions with Dr. Slonin first. He'll brief you about epidemiology which, we think, is the least complicated of the various scientific subjects to be debated during the convention." Roth scratched his chin. "It's also the subject most closely related to that facet of Nevsky's work, with which we are vitally concerned. You should be able to find a way of leading the conversation from epidemiology to germ warfare without arousing his suspicions. It's going to be tough. I know it, and you know it. Present him with several bottles of his favorite whiskey."

Baruch said, "It won't work."

Itzhak said, "We've got to think of more than that. Booze and music alone just won't do it."

Roth smiled. "You'll manage. You always do. We've set your date of departure—tentatively, mind you—for December fourth, when you'll proceed to Izmir, where your East German documents are being prepared. There, you'll change your appearance considerably before continuing on to Moscow on December sixth. That mustache of yours will also have to come off, Itzhak. I never liked it."

"*I* like it," Heidi said.

"Ah, the trials and tribulations of SB Agents living on the taxpayer's money," said Baruch.

"Did you read about Benjamin Schneider?"

The story was in all the papers. He was the youngest. He had died before his grandmother got him to the hospital.

"He was my nephew," said Baruch.

. . . 4

In Izmir, they were whisked away to a suburban villa, rented from a well-known Jewish leather goods merchant. He had been found sufficiently loyal and reliable, and he wouldn't ask unnecessary questions of his Israeli clients.

At the villa, a hairdresser and cosmetician flown from Tel Aviv especially for this purpose, set to work on them. Within twenty-four hours, the three Israeli agents had difficulty recognizing one another.

"Except in bed," said Heidi on the morning of their second day.

"You don't *see me* in bed," Baruch said.

"*I didn't mean you,*" Heidi told him.

"That remark wasn't necessary," said Itzhak.

Coincidentally, they had all been blonds. Heidi's hair had been a few shades darker than the men's, and more coppery. Now it was a deep auburn. The men's hair was jet black. The color of their eyes was also changed, with dark brown contact lenses for Heidi and Baruch, and pale blue for Itzhak.

More important than the change in their appearance—more likely than not, no one in Moscow would likely have recognized them as themselves—was the complete metamorphosis in their IDs, meticulously prepared and slightly creased East German identity cards and passports. Heidi's and Itzhak's identified Frau Ilse and Doctor Heinrich Schuehler, both born in, and residents of Leipzig.

Itzhak had additional identification as a graduate of the Pharmacological Faculty of Leipzig University, as well as a membership card of the East German Communist Party, dated 1949. Baruch's ID and scholastic qualifications were similar to Itzhak's, with a two-year age difference.

His new name was Fritz Hansel.

None of their names would stand up to thorough checking by Russian authorities, but there had been too little time to do a better job. They had, as a matter of course, been added to the Official List of Invited Foreign Participants with the help of a Jewish typist-secretary at Moscow State University, who was working for Security Branch.

All three had official invitations to the Eleventh Moscow International Scientific Research Convention, passes to the Moscow State University canteen, and free travel vouchers for the bus and tram lines of urban Moscow, valid from December 6 to December 15.

They were also equipped with a tourist roadmap of the city, and reservations at Hotel Berlin, from the afternoon of December 6, till noon December 16, ten days in which to befriend Professor Iliya Petrovitch Nevsky, and his wife, Vera, to attend a reasonable number of lectures (so as not to become too conspicuous by their absence), to gain admission to one of the Old Moscow University buildings on Mokhavaya Street (and, if possible, to the laboratories housed in its cellars), to find a few metal containers filled with a viscous fluid, in which billions of *Vibrio cholerae* bacilli 173 were stored—to implement the latest plot of genocide against Israel—and to destroy those containers, or to track their route to the Middle East.

"To tell you the truth, I'm scared," Heidi said.

"You're not alone," Baruch said. "Angry and scared."

"I'm not exactly filled with courage myself," said Itzhak.

Ten crowded days indeed, he pondered, as he and Heidi were in their bedroom later, Heidi trying on a long party dress—the first formal gown Itzhak had ever seen her wear.

They had all been fitted with complete new sets of clothing, from socks and handkerchiefs to winter overcoats made in East Germany, Czechoslovakia, Poland, and Hungary. Some of these clothes had actually been worn previously by agents traveling in Eastern Europe. Some had been artificially frayed and discolored. Only the formal dress Heidi was now trying on, and Itzhak's own black dinner suit, were new. They still had their Leipzig shop labels cleanly sewn into their linings. Heidi's gown was of a soft crimson material, and fitted her lush body beautifully.

"You look good enough to eat," Itzhak remarked.

"No bites," said Heidi, with a grin.

"It's marvelous. You stick out in exactly the right places. Everybody'll have eyes."

"They had my measurements exactly." She was pleased. "Your suits look good, too."

Itzhak was brooding again.

"What's wrong?" asked Heidi.

"Nothing's wrong," said Itzhak. "I suppose it's just nerves, not a real foreboding. And Baruch, poor man. His only nephew."

He rose and took Heidi in his arms, as though to reassure them both. He ran his hands all over her body. She thrust against him, and for a moment their breathing was heavy. Then she quickly pushed him away from their long embrace, whispering, "If anything should happen to you, I'd be finished too."

He chucked her under the chin. "Hush, baby, don't even say such a thing. We are one in body and soul. You just take good care of yourself, and no harm will come to me. I promise."

"Promises can be broken . . ."

"Not this promise. I want you to promise me something more, Heidi."

"What?"

"That if we're ever in a tight spot together, you'll obey me. That if anything goes wrong that I feel I can handle better on my own, you'll obey me without argument. When I say to you: 'Lehistalek'—that good Hebrew word which means to get out and disappear. Do you solemnly promise me that?"

"I promise," she replied.

. . . 5

A comfortable flight by a Turkish Airlines Caravelle took them to Leipzig, at midmorning on November 6.

Once there, they left through the normal "Returned Residents" exit.

Their first set of passports, which had been stamped with an outbound tourist visa a week earlier, passed the unhesitating inspection of immigration and police officers. There was nothing faulty there.

"I thought I saw a dubious frown on one of them," said Heidi.

"You're just anxious," Itzhak reassured her.

"Anxious, hell. I'm scared," Heidi said.

Once outside, Heidi and Itzhak turned in one direction and Baruch in another, with purposeful steps—as if they were going to a taxi stand, the airport bus stop, or to meet some acquaintance.

In fact, all they did was take a meandering walk, mingling with crowds of other travelers, and slowly working their way to the entrance gate for departing passengers.

Fortunately, this gate was far enough away from the other one, through which they had arrived some twenty minutes earlier.

"Moscow?" an attendant asked.

"Yes," said Itzhak.

They were booked on a flight due to leave in two hours.

For an hour more they wandered around inside the airport before they approached the Aeroflot ticket and baggage counter.

When they met there, in full view of Aeroflot officials and ground hostesses, they put on a fine show of friendship, delighted to meet by chance before departing on a visit abroad.

They approached the counter and asked for their tickets on the 12:30 Moscow flight.

Again, there seemed to be no hitches. But the Israelis were nervous and guarded.

They were able to pass into Customs and Immigration using their second set of East German passports, which showed that they had not traveled abroad for almost three years.

"Three years?" a flight officer exclaimed.

"Yes. It's a long time," Heidi told him.

"Many things have changed," he replied.

The Moscow plane took off on time. They kept their conversation to a minimum throughout the hour and a quarter flight that brought them to the Russian capital.

It had snowed most of the way, and visibility had been zero until just prior to the landing at Sheremetyevo International Airport, when their plane made a wide low circle over Moscow.

"Look! Just look at that!" Heidi exclaimed.

She was unable to contain her surprise and admiration.

The city, covered by a rather thin layer of snow, gleamed like an enormous crystal palace. The domes of Uspensky Cathedral were giant spun sugar hats in the well known and immediately recognizable mass of the Kremlin, which stood out against the vast expanse of Red Square. The Lenin Mausoleum and the Cathedral of Basil, the Beatified, flanked it to west and south.

"It's so beautiful, it makes you gasp," Heidi said.

"You're right, as always," Baruch said softly.

The Kutaigorod blocks of ministerial buildings could be seen to the east, and stately Gorki Street, running northward past the huge Dynamo Sports Stadium and the massive Council of Ministries. Cars and buses—slowly creeping along Lenin Prospekt, Sovietsky Boulevard, and Moscow's inimitable Sadovoyeh Ring, encompassing the entire City Center—looked like an endless convoy of black beatles, sharply contrasting with the still, silver band of the frozen Moskva River.

"It's so beautiful!" Heidi said.

All this below them, the ancient edifices, and immortal river, were overshadowed by the tall modern skyscrapers of the University (their destination on December 9), Hotel Leningrad, the Ministry of Foreign Affairs, the National Hotel, and others.

Everything surpassed in beauty and grandeur what Heidi and her companions had been expecting.

"What a marvelous view," she said.

"Better than Petah-Tiqva?" Itzhak teased, referring to one of Israel's least impressive little country towns.

Their arrival and processing was surprisingly quick. This made them uneasy. Especially Itzhak. When things went *too* smoothly, he was suspicious.

They were unable to decide whether it was just normal procedure, or if their official invitations to the convention had a direct bearing on their exceedingly efficient and polite passage through immigration and customs. None of their bags were searched. Obliging porters helped them effortlessly along to the exit and in to a taxi, whose driver whisked them off toward the city.

"What a relief." Baruch said in a low voice.

"My knees were shaking," said Heidi.

"We can't have any of that *yet*," Itzhak said. "This is only the beginning."

After passing farmhouses, villages, and old tenements—many of which had obviously been vacated and earmarked for demolition—they entered roads flanked by the high massive blocks of modern apartment houses.

Then, entering central Moscow from the north, they drove across impressive Sverdlov Square, with its beautiful palms, and along busy Okhotny Street. They drove down Mokhavaya Street, and briefly glimpsed the massive Lenin Library, but they didn't catch sight of the Old University Building, which lay further down toward Manyezh and the Kremlin.

The taxi driver was a fat fellow, whose red neck

folded out over his collar. He turned, and said, "You should be staying at the Hotel National, or Kiev."

He hesitated, then said, "Fine hotels with a good view. You can see the Kremlin from there. The Berlin isn't much."

Baruch gave a joking laugh, "We're just tourists, you know. We come from a socialist republic. We're not American or British capitalists."

Baruch caught the driver glancing at him in his overhead rearview mirror, and his eyes seemed more suspicious than those of the immigration authorities.

"You a Party member?" the driver asked.

"No. I'm not. My friend here is, but he can't speak Russian, and neither can his wife."

"All from East Germany?"

"Yeah. Leipzig."

The driver was silent for a time. Then he said, "Well, East Germans usually stay at the cheaper hotels. No tips, either."

"You're allowed to take tips?"

The driver chuckled, "Who asks? It's not a crime."

"Are there many tourists from the West?"

"Lots. But not in winter. Nice people, usually." He paused for a few moments. Then he said, "Money doesn't seem to have spoiled them." Then, "Here we are, comrade, Hotel Berlin. Have a pleasant holiday."

They nodded their thanks, and when Itzhak, who had understood nothing of their conversation in Russian, wanted to hand the driver a rather capitalist tip, Baruch pushed back his hand, and gave the driver about half as much—which was still more than he had expected from East Germans.

"We're playing it pretty close, if you ask me," Heidi said. "I don't like not being able to speak Russian."

"I'll take care of it, don't worry," said Baruch. "We'll get by."

Heidi shivered. "We'd better," she said.

The air was frigid in Moscow on December 6, 1972.

The three Israelis were very cold until they entered the hotel. But their small, rather austerely furnished hotel rooms were, if anything, overheated, and during their first leisurely hour of unpacking and settling in, they had even thrown open the double panes of their windows, to let in fresh air.

"I feel like an Eskimo! Bring me some furs," said Itzhak.

Heidi stood with her arms wrapped around herself.

Baruch closed the windows.

They had originally planned to hold their official discussions out of doors. They knew that their hotel rooms were, as likely as not, bugged, and that any attempt to remove hidden microphones, or even overtly search them out, would blow their cover.

"Out of doors" had sounded fine when discussed in Tel-Aviv at a temperature of 18 degrees Celsius above zero. Here in Moscow it was 8 below. A brisk stroll around the block in which Hotel Berlin was situated convinced them that they would have to find a different solution to their conference-site problem—one that included adequate heating.

"For God's sake! We should have brought battery heaters," Heidi said.

"That wouldn't have been a bad idea," said Baruch.

"We'll get used to it. We've *got* to get used to it," Itzhak said.

Small restaurants were out of the question, since they were always crowded and their tables very close. Conversation in German or English would at once attract attention.

Larger restaurants were very formal and utilitarian, with waitresses hovering over you, and all the staff apparently determined to keep you occupied with eating and drinking—from the moment you sat down until you were presented with the enormous bill.

"We've got to find something," Heidi said. "We'll just have to keep looking."

They ate sandwiches at a small standup bar, and returned to the hotel.

Time was at a premium. Itzhak and Baruch left the hotel again the same afternoon, taking different directions. Baruch headed for Manyezh Square and Mokhavaya Street, a route which would lead him past the Kremlin, and major public buildings, an area where his ability to read and understand the language would be an obvious advantage.

Itzhak scouted in the direction of one of Moscow's recreation and entertainment districts, and eventually found himself in Vorontzovskaya Road. A large and very very modern cinema attracted his attention, and he entered the glass and marble foyer.

He noted a spacious buffet with a bar, and half a dozen round glass-topped tables anchored to the floor.

The ticket booth faced the street, and the ticket seller had no way of watching the interior of the foyer. Entry to the cinema itself was by two ascending flights of stairs, curving about halfway up.

Itzhak stayed inside for almost a whole hour. No ushers came down the stairs. No one paid the slightest attention to him. Cinema-goers passed him by without stopping or even turning their heads.

This in itself was enough to increase his nervousness. Everything seemed strange and forbidding. Everybody seemed occupied with himself.

He drank two glasses of tea, and one measure of vodka. He smoked half a dozen cigarettes, went up the stairs to the curtained and closed entrances to the cinema auditorium, then back down to the underground rest rooms. He sat at the bar, then at one of the tables. And, so far as he could tell, he did not attract anyone's attention.

But he felt as if there were eyes in the walls. He did see one plainly dressed man in a gray coat and hat watching him, but the man turned and walked away, so Itzhak decided he was just strolling.

This, then, seemed as good a place as any to discuss their first practical steps, which must precede the convention opening on December 9, and perhaps devise the strategy that would facilitate their approach to Iliya and Vera Nevsky.

As Itzhak left the cinema, he was still unable to get the man in the gray overcoat out of his mind, and the terrible uneasy feeling that the walls held eyes.

. . . 6

That same evening, they met late at the cinema and sat at a central table, well away from the bar.

Baruch hunched over in his coat. He now wore a fur cap. "This seems like a strange place to meet," he said quietly in German.

"It is," Itzhak agreed. "But like I said, it's the best I could find. How was your reconnaissance?"

"Useless." said Baruch. "Utterly useless. Government offices, public institutions, libraries, hospitals, schools, all swarming with militia and plainclothes agents, no doubt. It's a beautiful city, though. But it's freezing cold. This place may be strange, but at least it's warm."

"You men with your warm underpants and woolen suits are so pitiful. What about a girl in a skirt and sheer nylon panty hose?" Heidi asked.

"I don't like panty hose," said Baruch.

"Why?" asked Itzhak.

"Well, it's sort of a secret," Baruch said.

"I bet I know, but I won't tell," Heidi said.

Itzhak broke in, "If we are through discussing the hazards of the Russian climate, and panty hose, I suggest we get down to business."

Heidi nodded, and Baruch became serious.

Itzhak said, "The two subjects are the convention, and a professor we shall call Ny—by using the letters at the beginning and end of his last name. Convention registration begins day after tomorrow, a day before the official opening on the ninth. We can't afford wasting those two days."

He turned to Baruch. "We have Ny's address. I

think that you, Fritz, should make the first move. Why not phone Ny, say you just arrived from Leipzig together with other convention delegates, and would like to make the acquaintance of a scientist whose name and work has been mentioned to you. You're young enough to make it sound like a case of hero worship."

Baruch shook his head. "We've got to do some more thinking. Assuming Ny goes for that bit of flattery, isn't he likely to steer me into a highly scientific discussion, during which my flimsy cover will soon become transparent to a man like him?"

"I've given some thought to that, Fritz. Let's take him by storm. By surprise. I think Ilse and I should come along wherever you're going to meet him. We'll, of course, apologize profusely for tagging along uninvited. And you can easily explain that we ran into each other, just as you were leaving the hotel, and that you felt sure Ny wouldn't mind meeting a scientist friend of yours. Once we're all together, Ilse and I will help keep you away from superscientific subjects."

Baruch stared at the table morosely. "What makes you so sure Ny will invite me at all, Heinrich?"

"Because, my dear Fritz, Russian intelligenstia is renowned for its hospitality. It's about the only characteristic they have in common with the proletariat."

"Well I hope to hell you're right, Heinrich," Heidi said. "And I also hope to hell that this also holds true for the wives of Russian scientists."

Itzhak sighed. "We can but try, Ilse. We can but try." He turned and looked around them. "Now, how about a lemon tea and a drop of vodka?"

When they had emptied their glasses, Baruch walked over to the main entrance, and bought three tickets for the continuous show. They went inside, and watched half of a well acted, but overly dramatized film, about a Russian submarine crew serving in Arctic waters.

Outside again, Heidi turned to Itzhak. "I don't think much of their movies."

"Give them another chance."

Heidi surreptitiously took Itzhak's hand and scratched his palm. He smiled down at her. Then he gave her a hefty slap on the behind. She bridled, as women will, but her eyes were bright.

They all returned to the Hotel Berlin together, and went to their rooms for an early night's sleep, wondering how much sleep they would get during the next twelve days.

Alone in his room, Baruch was restless. He had a sudden notion. He bundled up and went out of the hotel to the nearest library. There, he spent an hour boning up on material that might interest Nevsky. He would post Heidi and Itzhak on what he had learned. Even here at the library, he still felt that he was followed, that he was being watched.

He knew that this must be the feeling of many Russian people.

Baruch called Professor Nevsky at nine o'clock in the morning on December 7th, from outside the hotel, but was too late to reach him.

He had thought this too *early* an hour, not being aware of the professor's daily rising habits. But he had been mistaken. This made him feel no better. Vera Nevskaya had answered the phone. "The professor isn't here. He already left for the university. But he'll be home by one o'clock. Who is calling?"

Baruch hesitated. Then he said, "Just a visitor."

Vera Nevsky was immediately curious. "Come, come! Who is this, please? If you'll just leave your name, I'll have him call you when he returns. I'll make a note of it."

"It's of no importance. I'll call again later."

Vera Nevsky put into her voice almost a note of tenderness. "Iliya would call you, I'm sure."

Baruch said, "Thank you. I'll call him," and hung up.

There. He had done it. It was abrupt, the way he had wanted. It would make them wonder. He could apologize later. He returned to the hotel and went to his room. He remained there throughout the forenoon. He was certain that Vera Nevsky in the meantime, had somehow contacted her husband. They would both be wondering. Her concern would be appeased when he finally talked with Nevsky.

Every little bit helped.

At 11:30, he phoned Nevsky's home once again. The bell rang and rang, and Baruch was about to replace the receiver when finally, a pleasant male voice answered in Russian: "Yes?"

"This is Fritz Hansel," Baruch said.

"Herr Fritz Hansel?" The Russian had used the German "Herr."

"Yes," Baruch replied in German, his heart missing a beat. "Am I speaking to Professor Nevsky?"

"You are. I am Iliya Petrovitch Nevsky." The professor had sounded slightly irritated at first but his voice began to smooth out. "I've just spoken to my wife. She called me at work, and said someone had phoned. Was it you?" His German was faultless.

"It was I, Professor. I'm very sorry indeed, and profoundly grateful that you took the trouble, in the middle of your important work to answer."

Now the professor was abrupt. "And what can I do for you, Herr Hansel?"

"I should be most honored to meet you, Herr Professor. I'm here with other convention delegates."

Now the professor relaxed. "Ah—I see," he said. "I am lecturing at the convention. We could meet then."

"Of course, Herr Professor. But I'll be leaving for Moscow soon after the end of the convention, and I thought we might be less busy these coming two days prior to the opening."

There was a long silence at the other end of the line, then the voice of the professor came very slowly. "That is true, Herr Hansel. Tell me, who has told you about me? Is there some special reason why you should want to see me so suddenly? So urgently?"

Baruch replied, "Your name and work in epidemiology have been repeatedly mentioned to those of us working in the same field. Of course, we're in other fields too. Leipzig University, small and insignificant though it is compared to yours in Moscow, is fully aware of the great men in scientific research. It's only natural, therefore, that I should wish to meet you, Professor Nevsky. You must forgive my impatience. I should have explained to your wife who I am. Please ask her to forgive me."

"Good, good, Herr Hansel. I understand, and appreciate your compliment. I suppose you heard about me through Dr. Staniev, who is one of your Leipzig lecturers, I believe."

This was just the sort of question Baruch most feared. Of course, the name Staniev was completely new to him, but his reply had to be unequivocal. He could only hope Nevsky would not check back with Staniev during the coming twelve days. That was the calculated risk he had to take. He found himself perspiring.

"Yes, Professor. Dr. Staniev is one of those who sings your praises . . . Though by no means the only one."

"Thank you again, Herr Hansel. Well now, let me see. Today is Thursday, the seventh. The convention opens Saturday. Tomorrow my calendar is rather crowded. What are your plans for this evening? Are you alone?"

Baruch jumped at this unexpected opportunity, and said, "Actually, this evening I have been asked to join a fellow scientist, a friend of mine from Leipzig, Heinrich Schuehler, who is also attending the convention. We thought of going out for supper with his wife."

"His wife . . . Ah, let me see. Vera—that is, my wife—loves to speak German. And she has so little opportunity for practice. Why don't you let me call her and see whether she could fix us all up with a light supper at our house. It would be my pleasure, I assure you."

"But no," Baruch protested loudly, while he hoped he was not overdoing it. "I could not impose upon you and your gracious wife all this trouble." There was a silence. He thought about Professor Nevsky quickly. The man's voice was soft, gentle, with anything but the powerful commanding tones he had expected.

"Nonsense, Herr Hansel. We're alone together too

often in the evening. As for Vera, she will be delighted with my proposal, if it doesn't come too late; I'd better speak to her at once. Please stay by your phone and I'll call back within a quarter of an hour."

Baruch again protested, weakly, and finally accepted. By noon, his phone rang. They were, all three, invited for eight o'clock. Iliya Nevsky jokingly warned that it would only be a very light meal—no American steaks, or English meat pies. A spot of sea-lox and caviar—perhaps a little kasha too.

Baruch had other arrangements in his mind, but he did not voice them at this moment.

He said, "Not all of us Germans eat sausages with saurerkraut before going to bed," he reassured the professor. "As for drinks, you must allow us to be the providers."

"This will certainly be a pleasure," the professor said.

"I hope so, sir," Baruch said. "It's been my ambition to meet you for a long time."

Vera Danilova had been a featured dancer with the Bolshoi Ballet when Iliya Petrovitch Nevsky first laid eyes on her. A young scientist then, he was seated in the last row of the balcony at a performance of *Swan Lake* when she caught his eye.

He watched her through his opera glasses, following every movement of her body. He had never seen anyone so graceful, so beautiful. By the time she took her curtain call, his heart was beating like a drum.

For three weeks he had bought tickets to every ballet she danced in, tickets that cost him more and more as he advanced nearer to the stage. He couldn't afford the cost of the tickets, but he had to get closer to her. For three weeks, he knew no other way.

Finally, he knew he had to meet her. He began to send tiny little bouquets to her dressing room, signing the card inside: "Your very grateful admirer, Iliya P. Nevsky." With the fourth bouquet, he sent a longer note, telling Vera that he was a young scientist, describing his features, and asking her if she could perhaps smile at him when she left the stage door that night.

He would be waiting outside.

Iliya Nevsky had been very nervous as he waited. When she walked through the door, he was almost breathless.

She was with another ballerina, laughing and talking, and Iliya was certain that she would ignore him. When she suddenly looked up and caught his eye, she stared for a moment without expression. Then a very faint, almost imperceptible smile had crossed her face before she turned back to speak to the girl she was with.

Iliya Nevsky began waiting patiently every night outside the stage door. They were both painfully shy, and it was weeks before he had the courage to speak. And when Vera Danilova had spoken in return, it was in a voice so low he could barely understand what she said.

"I am very happy to meet you." Those were her words, and they made him a brave man. He asked permission to accompany her to the door of her house, and she gave it.

Much of the trip had been spent in silence. But three nights later, when they made the same trip, they began a gentle conversation, then another. Inside a month, they were in love.

It had taken Iliya Nevsky two years to earn enough money to ask Vera to marry him. Though she was on the verge of becoming a prima ballerina, she said yes at once.

An only child himself, Iliya Nevsky had wanted heirs. Vera, too, wanted a family. But the family never came. The sons her husband longed for, the daughters, had never reached conception.

It had saddened them, but not diminished their love. To Vera, Iliya was the kindest, most solicitous of men. To Iliya, Vera would always be the beautiful swan he had seen on the Bolshoi stage, transformed by his love into a woman.

After calling Professor Nevsky, Baruch went to visit Itzhak and Heidi.

Itzhak answered the door. Heidi was sitting on the bed with her legs crossed.

Baruch had a hard time keeping his eyes off Heidi. He tried to focus on Itzhak. He told them of their dinner invitation.

"Fritz, you really are a magician," Heidi said. She had retreated to the bathroom.

"I absolutely agree with Ilse," Itzhak said. "What a great honor! Thank you, Fritz, for inviting us to come along."

"You should write poetry," said Baruch.

Itzhak chuckled.

"He was most insistent that I bring you, Heinrich. He also mentioned how pleased his wife would be to have Ilse to chat with in German."

"I'll tell her all about the latest fashions in Berlin," said Heidi, "while you men discuss science."

"I think we should take them out to dinner," said Baruch. "If you think about it, we've put them on the spot, and I think we should do the entertaining."

"Terrific," said Itzhak.

Baruch said, "I went to the library to bone up. I found a good restaurant with live music. They even have a special virtuoso who plays the violin. I thought we'd take them there. We'll go to his house first and then to the restaurant. It's a nice place. I looked in."

Heidi got off the bed and stretched.

"I'll call the professor now," Baruch said quickly. "To keep them from preparing to feed us all."

Baruch beat a hasty retreat. Sometimes he thought Heidi was provocative on purpose.

. . . 7

Gorkova Prospekt had class.

The invited Israeli agents arrived by taxi, bringing two bottles of whiskey and a dozen hothouse roses—for which they had had to pay five times as much as for the duty-free liquor.

Iliya Nevsky opened the door. He wore a short wool coat, a pair of baggy flannels, and loafers with thin leather soles.

He looked his age. His hair was gray, unruly, and bushy. He had a large bald circle in the middle, which the Israelis would have called, Ben Gurionic. The professor had dark skin, indicative of his Georgian descent. He was short and square in build, though by no means stout. His movements displayed marked gravity. He welcomed them in German.

"We're delighted to meet you, Professor," said Baruch, and made the proper introductions.

The Professor led them into a homely living room, furnished with old but elegant furniture, including a massive sideboard, that bore the signs of many years of use. There was the smell of a burning fireplace in the room, but the temperature was chilly, even with the fire.

"My wife will join us soon, Frau Schuehler. She insists on trying to make herself more beautiful than she is—which in my opinion is not only impossible but unnecessary."

Heidi turned to Itzhak and smiled. She said, "Please, Heinrich, take a lesson from Professor Nevsky on how to flatter your wife."

"Frau Schuehler would fully justify the most extravagant flattery," the professor said.

Heidi was obviously flattered. "Thank you," she said. "You are very kind."

Nevsky took the whiskey, and put it on the sideboard.

The professor walked with a slouch, and slowly. His hair was as fine as silk.

As he stood at the sideboard, he asked: "A drink? My wife won't mind if we have one before she joins us. She's not as much of a drinker as her husband."

Nevsky poured straight whiskey into glasses, filling them to the brim.

"We imagined that visitors were inevitably offered vodka," said Baruch.

"A bourgeois concept, I assure you, Herr Hansel. Our educated class are not Nationalists in their appreciation of good food and drink." He seemed polite in every way.

"The roses are beautiful," he continued. "Roses are too frail for Russia—at least for Moscow, but Vera loves them. She claims my preoccupation with viruses and bacteria carries with it a permanent antiseptic odor. For that reason, she insists on buying aromatic plants. Of course, she's right. There's a laboratory smell that gets into one's clothes, and possibly even into the hair—what hair I have left . . ." He rubbed the bald spot on his head with his fingers. "However, we should not blame innocent little germs for that, but rather the germicide and disinfectant chemicals we insist on using."

"Ilse loathes *my* laboratory smell, if that's any comfort to you, Professor," said Itzhak.

"It's repugnant," said Heidi. She put her fingers to her nose and gently squeezed as she smiled.

Vera Nevsky was entering the room. She still had the beauty, the grace of a swan.

The professor turned abruptly. "Ah, here you are, my dear." He smiled and made the introductions.

Vera Nevsky said, "Did I overhear a discussion about the smells of the laboratory?"

"Indeed you did," said Heidi. "The gentlemen were disparaging our fine sense of smell."

Vera Nevsky looked rueful. "Yes," she said, "it's one of the hazards of marrying a scientist." She smiled warmly at her husband.

Baruch explained that they were going to a restaurant called the Explosion. Vera Nevsky threw her hands up in dismay, looking toward her husband. But when she saw the way his eyes twinkled, and the way he smiled, she smiled again too. "All right. That will be lovely. We'll go with you, but we insist on taking you in our car."

"That's very kind of you," Itzhak said. He was watching the professor.

Nevsky had refilled his glass with whiskey to the brim, and had chugalugged the entire glassful.

Iliya Nevsky drove a long black Volga limousine, but he seemed apologetic about using the car. It was comfortable, and he drove fast.

"This is what we ride in," he said. "I use it every day at the office. It impresses people. My superiors would dislike my taking a taxi." It wasn't long before they were parked in a dark, forbidding-looking alley near a door that glistened with black paint. Over the door was a simple red ball, with extended orange spokes, which represented fire. This was the entrance to the Explosion.

"Here we are," said Nevsky.

Inside, it was opulent and dimly lit. There were heavy black and crimson draperies, all of velvet, brocaded and embroidered in gold. The tables were not close together. The carpets were deep red plush. Sublime violin music was being played. The violinist was a man in a golden robe.

"Listen to that! Listen!" Iliya Nevsky said as they waited for a table. "It's all improvisation. Every bit of it. I come here quite frequently. Vera doesn't like it. Do you Vera?"

"It's not that I don't like it. Iliya. It's just that I

don't think that a man of your standing should come here so often."

"My standing!" the Professor said, as if it were nothing.

A slim pale-faced man in black Cossack pants and a red velvet jacket, came toward them. "Five?" he asked.

Baruch nodded.

"Come with me."

They followed him to a table near a column draped in black velvet and sat down.

"The food is excellent here," Iliya said. "Isn't it, Vera?" She had risen to stand behind Nevsky's chair, to smooth his hair. Then she went to her chair and sat down again, looking at him with a fond smile. "Yes, it is," she said.

Now that they were settled, Baruch—and Itzhak, in turn—began to speak of Nevsky's research in epidemiology. Most of the Israelis' questions were of a general nature, and received full answers, but when Itzhak referred specifically to cholera, Nevsky became much more vague than he had been so far, though without the slightest apparent sign of suspicion.

Their wine came first. This was followed by a wheeled cart, served by three men. The food was first-rate, the china was Rosenthal. It was far more luxurious than the Israelis had expected. And during the course of the meal, they had ample time to observe the professor's beautiful wife.

Vera Nevsky was taller than Iliya, and inclined to mother him, even here at the Explosion. Nevsky sat, as was his habit, on the edge of his chair.

Vera had long, black and naturally wavy hair. It fell loosely over her slender shoulders, which were exposed except for two narrow straps holding up a low-cut gown of gleaming black, cut to reveal her magnificent figure. Every movement she made was graceful.

The perfect whiteness of her skin was luminous. It was enhanced by her black dress and hair. Her face was a sculptor's ideal, with pronounced cheekbones, a rather long, aquiline nose, and nostrils that contracted and dialated with each breath. Over her soft, delicately chiseled chin, she had a wide mouth, whose lips often remained slightly apart, lending to her an expression of expectancy. Her overlarge eyes, dark and glistening were rarely still—dancing from speaker to speaker, and flashing gratefully at any word of kindness, appreciation, or flattery, whether directed toward herself, or Nevsky. And there were many such words spoken at that night's supper at the Explosion.

Over coffee and brandy, Baruch succeeded in carefully guiding the conversation to epidemiological research. The professor had returned to his bottle of vodka, which he had ordered along with his meal. And after one or two attempts by his wife to discourage him, he was permitted to drink more heavily than he should have. Each glassful was drunk immediately to the bottom, in the Russian manner.

Heidi and Vera were drawn together and talked closely, while the men spoke of science.

It was surprising how far Baruch's information—recently memorized from a few concise books—could go, especially when the host was becoming expansive, with two-thirds of a bottle of good vodka in his veins.

Nevsky was also very attentive to the music. As he drank, he listened, smiling at his wife, as though she were dancing to the violin.

Itzhak and Baruch sounded Nevsky out on his views concerning the situation in the Middle East and, to their relief, discovered him to be much less bigoted and onesided than they had expected.

More than that, Professor Nevsky appeared almost completely disinterested in the Arab-Israeli conflict. Both of his guests endeavored to find out whether this indifference was studied or real. And both, when they compared impressions later, were in full agreement: the professor had no ideological axes to grind, no anti-Israel sentiments, and not a trace of anti-semitism. Indeed, if anything, Nevsky appeared to like Jews very much, with a high degree of respect for their intellectual endeavor and devotion to the sciences.

The majority of his own teachers at the State University had been Jewish.

Nevsky proudly overemphasized this fact, even under the impression that he was addressing pure Aryan Germans. In fact, he sounded *them* out, and was glad to find Itzhak and Baruch wholly unaffected by the worm of Jew-hatred, which had never died, and was again "rearing its ugly head" in German schools.

"The worm, yes the worm, rearing its ugly head," Nevsky said.

When at last they managed to get the conversation back to science, the professor said, "It's really good to see young men like you going into research. We're living in a coldblooded, materialistic world, which does not take time out for learning, or work that is not of a directly lucrative nature."

Nevsky continued. "Our social structure is undoubtedly superior to any other in the world, particularly in these past few years since the demise of the personality cult."

"Yes, Herr Professor—" Baruch began.

"Iliya, my dear Fritz."

"Yes, Iliya. You're a great nation in the arts and sciences of peace, but your great cultural and social achievements will again and again be threatened by the capitalist warmongers. The Germans will conspire to destroy these achievements. They're doing so right now, I have no doubt," Baruch went on. "It is, therefore, encumbent upon Russia that it build and maintain effective defense systems, which will prove impregnable to any enemy attack."

Had he gone too far, Baruch wondered.

Itzhak, too, was momentarily concerned.

Professor Nevsky looked up from his glass and stared into Baruch's eyes.

Then, as if he had satisfied himself on an important point, he picked up his drink and again chugalugged. He looked at the empty glass and bottle. Without saying a word, he signaled a waiter, who came running at once with another bottle.

"Hostraley plays well tonight," said Nevsky.

"Hostraley plays well every night," the waiter said.

Itzhak decided it was his turn. "The Americans have

been using gas in Vietnam, a weapon even Hitler didn't use. And not only gases. Americans have killed the rice crops in communist-controlled zones of Vietnam, Laos, and Cambodia. They may even have resorted to germ warfare."

He felt a sinking sensation in his stomach. But this dart went home. The professor sat up straight and said, "Mother Russia will not be the aggressor, but neither will she allow herself to become the victim. You may rest assured of that!"

The alcohol the professor had drunk had, amazingly, caused no discernable reaction.

"But is there a perfect defense against unconventional weapons?"

"My dear Heinrich, I am no military expert. And even if I were you would not expect me to betray my country's secrets, even to loyal East German friends."

"Certainly not," Baruch said. "Heinrich only meant that he hopes—we all hope—that great scientists like you will find a way to neutralize the enemy's war preparations, which we fear include stockpiles of gases and chemicals." His stomach tightened. "Possibly including germs that have not been used openly in any previous wars."

"We must put our trust in the government, and in our excellent Generals," said the professor. "Of course, there may very well be germ weapons against which the only potent defense is the production and stockpiling of identical weaponry.

Now, he had said it. Both Itzhak and Baruch looked intently at Nevsky. Was he aware of how close he was coming to what would amount to the betrayal of classified information? Would he, in the morning, perhaps—when the effects of the alcohol had worn off—become conscious of having been manipulated?

Baruch decided on one more ploy. They would probably not meet again under such congenial and advantageous circumstances.

"That sounds logical. That system has, in all probability, already saved the world from nuclear warfare. Had we lagged behind in our production of nuclear weapons, and our stockpiling of fissionable materials, we might have been destroyed. It stands to reason that leading scientists do their share in preparing the necessary materials of chemical or germ warfare." He hesitated, "If we are doing so in a democratic republic, I, for one, would be prepared to volunteer to contribute whatever I can—gratis."

"Well," Nevsky smiled with a kind of mischief in his eyes. "Who knows but what it might not be arranged. I might have a word with my old friend, Doctor Staniev. I can't promise you anything, mind you, but I like to encourage young scientists like you, and the paramilitary field is—unhappily—the best-endowed nowadays, in most countries."

He again poured his glass full of vodka. "Presumably, also in yours. And money is the indespensable fuel without which no laboratory worth its salt can function. Maybe—*maybe,* before you leave Moscow, we should get together again and talk about this. But, ah, we must not forget the ladies."

He looked directly at Heidi, and then more softly at his wife.

Itzhak looked up. He caught a man's eye. The man did not wear the gray coat, the gray hat, that he had worn at the cinema earlier. He was dressed in brown now, with a black scarf. But it was the same face.

. . . 8

Heidi and Vera displayed all the evidence of having struck up an instantaneous friendship.

"You have the most charming and clever young wife," Vera remarked to Itzhak.

"And I may say as much, and more, about Vera," said Heidi to Iliya Nevsky.

"Thank you, Frau Schuehler. We must all meet again soon."

"That has already been arranged," said Vera. "We are going sightseeing and shopping tomorrow, and having lunch at that lovely Georgian restaurant I told you about. I'll take Ilse to GUM's and then to Red Square."

"By all means, dearest," the professor said. "That is—if Heinrich has no objections."

"Women rule the world, Iliya," said Itzhak. "Who are we to say no to them?"

"That's settled then," Baruch said. "May the lone bachelor here suggest that we call it a night?"

"I'll drive you back," the professor said—somewhat to their alarm. They doubted his ability to drive safely.

But once behind the wheel of the long Volga limousine, Iliya Nevsky seemed absolutely sober.

When Nevsky and his wife had dropped them off at the hotel entrance, Itzhak remarked quietly, "Good work, Baruch. With a bit of luck like tonight's, we'll get inside the institute yet." But, he said it dryly. He was still worried about the man in the brown coat . . . among other things.

"Nevsky certainly doesn't look like an Al Fatah Liberation Front sympathizer," said Heidi, on their way to their rooms.

"According to my book, he definitely isn't," Itzhak said.

"I agree," added Baruch. "I'll be willing to bet that he hasn't any idea that he's helping to produce germ-pollution materials for Habbash or Iyad. He probably thinks that it's all for their own defense systems!"

"And that, my dear Herr Hansel, may well be the bomb with which we shall explode the plans of our foes," Itzhak said with a smile.

A small car labored down the street, and parked directly in front of Iliya Nevsky's home. A man in a brown overcoat and a black scarf got out and slammed the door. He drew the scarf more tightly around his neck then walked directly to the door and knocked.

Vera Nevsky opened the door. "Yes? What is it?" she asked, staring at the man. He had a round face, with a thin-lipped mouth and piercing blue eyes. His nose was very red. He took off his hat. Then he said, "KGB."

Vera Nevsky showed not the least embarrassment. She said, "Won't you come in?"

"Yes."

The man stalked into the room.

Professor Nevsky turned from poking the fire in the grate, and asked, "Who is it, Vera?"

"A . . . man."

"You've been out with some strangers," the man said.

"That's true," Nevsky said. "They're Germans. From Leipzig. Why are you concerned?"

The man reached into his coat, hauled out a leather folder, opened it, and held it before Nevsky's eyes.

Nevsky's eyebrows lifted.

"Now I see," he said slowly. "Are the East Germans suspected of anything?"

"That's what I'm trying to find out," the man said.

"What is your name?" Nevsky said.

"Genovitch Statro. Of what did you speak with the East Germans?"

"We merely discussed general things," Nevsky replied.

"General?" asked the man.

He had been with the KGB only two months. He was already ambitious for a higher rank. He imagined that if he could do something big by himself, it would mean a great deal. He knew that if someone else took over, he would be alone again in the cold of this Russian city, walking the streets and accomplishing nothing. If it hadn't been for the suspicious actions of the man at the cinema, he would have had nothing to show for his efforts. He had been on his trail ever since seeing him. He had followed orders . . . and he had drunk nothing but water at the Explosion.

"You were at a night club," he said.

Nevsky shrugged. "So?"

"You say you talked with these people?"

"Yes. *Talked*. And sat. And drank. With my wife and another woman and two other men. Yes. Is that all?"

"You needn't act superior with me, Professor. I know who you are."

"Then why do you act this way?" The professor's hands were trembling. This intrusion was too much for him to bear calmly. He had never before had anything like this happen. It was untoward and unjustified. Inwardly, he cursed the man.

"I could have you both arrested on suspicion," the KGB man said.

The professor was in a rage now. "Just try it," he said, "and see what happens."

Statro was sobered, but still persistent. "You say you talked. How do I know what you talked about? How do I know who they are?"

"Get out! Get out of this house! Get out before I throw you out!" Nevsky was enraged.

Statro put on his hat. He turned, opened the door himself, and left. He drove directly to the Hotel Berlin, holding an inner monologue with himself that would have driven a saner man crazy. Actually, he was not responsible for his actions at this moment. His thoughts were incoherent. They were a mixture of Professor Nevsky, of the night club, of the people he had seen there, and of the words that he had not heard.

It had never once entered his mind that he could be wrong.

Inside the Hotel Berlin, Statro flashed his credentials to the desk clerk and went up in the elevator. He hesitated in front of Itzhak and Heidi's room. He did not knock.

He knew that if he entered, he would be facing two people.

He had followed Itzhak here before.

He knew where Baruch's room was . . . That's where he should go.

For a long time Statro stood in front of Baruch's door.

He could hear movements inside. Someone was pacing the floor. Back and forth, back and forth.

Somewhere, in a book on criminology, Statro had read that this was a good time to strike.

. . . 9

Inside his room, Baruch was pondering a number of things.

There had been times when Itzhak had seemed preoccupied. Why?

How could a man so slight and seemingly gentle as Nevsky down the quantities of liquor he did and show no sign? Was it a Russian aptitude? Or just an individual characteristic?

If Baruch had drunk as much as Nevsky, they'd have had to carry him out of the Explosion.

He could still hear the violin music.

He hated violins. The sound made his ears ring. Even at the thought of it, he rubbed his ears with both hands.

He thought of Heidi. Heidi and Itzhak. They would be there, in their room on the floor below him, lying on the bed, probably naked, making love.

He needed a girl. He wondered if he could get one if he phoned the desk clerk. He wondered if he could get one by walking the streets, but he also knew it wasn't a wise idea.

He had locked his door. He was facing the windows, rocking on his heels.

He heard the door being opened. He whirled around quickly.

"You're coming with me," said Statro.

Baruch laughed outright. He doubled up with laughter. As he laughed, he walked toward the man. Statro's brown hat was pulled low over his eyes, and it seemed to Baruch that he had seen him someplace before, but he couldn't decide where. It was a moon-face, with narrow eyes—but the eyes were not naturally narrow. They were tensed that way to frighten, to scare.

This only made Baruch laugh harder.

"What the hell's the matter with you?" Statro asked.

"You! *You!*" Baruch said, gasping.

Statro was taken aback. He didn't know what to do. If he fired and killed Baruch in this room, he would have a lot of explaining to do. And maybe, it would be the wrong thing. He wasn't sure.

Baruch knew this.

"Come with me," Statro said.

"Can't you at least show me some credentials?" Baruch asked.

The KGB man seemed to consider. He reached in his pocket, and pulled out the brown leather folder. Baruch approached even closer. He saw that Statro was with the Russian police.

"So!" Baruch said. "Why are you here?"

"You'll know soon enough," Statro said. "Come along."

There was nothing else to do, but Baruch was already planning his strategy. He knew that if he got into the wrong hands now, everything would be blown. Even Professor Nevsky would be in trouble. The Russian police had far-reaching tentacles.

"All right," he said.

Statro stepped aside, still holding the automatic, and Baruch preceded him.

"We're going down to see your friends now," Statro said.

"What friends?" Baruch said.

"You know what friends," Statro said.

"But I have no friends in this hotel," Baruch said.

"Liar!" said Statro. He rammed his gun into Baruch's back.

This was a mistake, but Baruch did not take advantage of it. He walked on down the hall.

The KGB man walked closely beside him, pointing the gun in Baruch's direction. They came to the elevator. Statro pressed the button.

It was now that Baruch acted.

Statro had looked toward the elevator button as he pressed it. His eyes were averted, the gun pointed slightly awry.

Baruch came down with a hard judo chop, and the gun clattered onto the floor. Statro shouted something in Russian that Baruch did not understand, and fumbled for the gun. Baruch got to it before Statro. He picked it up swiftly, and struck Statro on the chin with the barrel. He struck him again and again.

"You don't have to do that!" Statro moaned.

"But I'm doing it anyway!"

"Don't shoot me."

"Why not?" Baruch laughed. "Here's the elevator now." The doors opened. "Get inside!"

Statro hesitated.

Baruch brought the Browning automatic swiftly across the man's face, hooking against his nose and leaving a bloody gash. Blood dripped. Tears sprang into Statro's eyes.

"Get into the elevator!" Baruch said.

Statro got into the elevator, and huddled in the corner.

Baruch stepped up to him, and whipped the gun across his face again. Statro's hat fell off.

"Please don't do this. *Please!*" said Statro. He licked his lips. "You're going to kill me, aren't you?"

"I haven't yet decided," Baruch said.

Statro stared at him, one eye gushing blood. He licked his lips again.

"You like the taste of blood?" asked Baruch.

"No."

"Then why are you licking it?"

"Because I . . . I . . ."

"You can't even talk, can you?" Baruch said, ramming the gun into the man's gut. "I know this gun. This is a Browning Parabella automatic. It's a hefty gun for a man like you."

The elevator stopped and the doors came open.

"Outside now," Baruch said. Statro didn't hesitate. He walked out of the elevator into the basement, which was empty and dark, with only dim yellow bulbs hanging from the ceiling.

Baruch knew this man, as he knew every man. He rammed the gun hard into Statro's back. "Go toward the rear door there, the steel one. See it? With the red light?"

"I see it," said Statro.

"Walk like the man you are," Baruch said. "You haven't got any guts, have you?"

"No," Statro said sadly. He walked slowly toward the door.

Baruch opened the cellar door, and they went out into a dark alley. Baruch closed the door. For a moment they stood there facing each other.

"Now comes the moment that all men face," Baruch said.

"What do you mean?" Statro said.

"You don't even know that, do you?"

"No. I guess I don't."

"You had such high hopes, didn't you," Baruch said.

"High hopes," the man repeated, like a robot.

"Turn and walk back down the alley toward the wall there," Baruch said.

The man shuffled along the alley. It was very cold. Baruch could feel the chill. He wished this hadn't happened. But it had, and there was nothing he could do about it. He knew that both Roth and Boran would approve of what he was doing. The KGB man would be found the near the Hotel Berlin.

KGB men were found dead all over the place, probablv, and other men, too, that KGB men had killed.

They came to the end of the alley, and the man turned and faced Baruch.

Baruch looked at him. "I don't even know your name, and I don't want to know your name," he said.

Statro rubbed his chin.

Baruch shot. He pulled the trigger on the Browning automatic, and sent four Parabellum slugs into the man's face. The KGB man stood there for a moment, spouting more blood, and then he dropped like a rock.

Baruch wiped his fingerprints off the gun, turned,

and ran across the floor toward the elevator door. Moments later, he was inside his room, and there was silence once again. He looked in the mirror.

His hair was disheveled. He combed it. He turned, and let himself out of the door, locking it securely. He took the elevator down to Itzhak and Heidi's room, and knocked on the door. They had to be told.

Heidi, in a blue wrapper, answered the door.

"Baruch!" she said.

"Let me in. Please!"

She stood aside, and he entered the room.

Itzhak was wearing a red woolen robe, holding it tightly at the waist.

Baruch held a finger to his lips, asking for silence. The walls must not overhear.

Carefully, taking a sheet of paper and a pencil, he wrote down what he had done and why.

Later, none of them heard an alarm on the death of the KGB man. It was as if he had vanished into limbo. They suspected that the Russian police would want it that way.

. . . 10

During the morning of Friday, December 8, Heidi and Itzhak—followed an hour later by Baruch—went to Moscow State University to register for the convention.

Their names were checked on the official list of delegates from East Germany, and a uniformed hostess smiled at them.

"Where are you staying?" she asked Heidi and Itzhak.

They told her.

"Are you enjoying your visit?"

"Oh, yes," said Heidi.

"Do you like Moscow?"

"We've never visited a finer city."

They received a printed program, listing the lectures, symposia, and workshop discussion groups, and they noted that Iliya Petrovitch Nevsky was to head the group on epidemiology. There were also invitations to sightseeing tours to the Lenin Mausoleum, the Park of Culture, and the Tretyakov Art Gallery, as well as a complimentery admission voucher to the Bolshoi Theater.

When they later met in Sverdlov Square, Baruch said, "Our hosts certainly do these things in style, don't they?"

"It's great," Itzhak said. "We'll have to come back sometime for a real holiday."

Heidi tugged at Itzhak's arm. "And stay over there," she said, pointing in the direction of the nearby, monumental Moskava Hotel.

It had begun to snow, and the three commandos made their way to a restaurant on Okhotniy Road.

When they had ordered, Baruch asked Heidi about her afternoon shopping plans with Vera Nevsky. Heidi was to meet her at three, outside the Komsomolskaya Metro Station.

"I think we're all beginning to feel quite at home, Ilse," said Itzhak.

"I got all A's in map reading," she said.

Baruch looked around the restaurant. Then his eyes touched his companions. "OK, Heinrich, what's our next step?" he asked.

"A meeting in the Vorontzovskaya Cinema foyer at five. We'll stay there till about six, Ilse, if you're able to join us. If not, then back to the hotel. Perhaps Ny will contact us this evening."

"Do everything you can to arrange another meeting for us soon, Ilse," Baruch said.

"I've thought about that, Fritz. Why not invite them over for dinner at that nice restaurant we saw near the Berlin?"

"Terrific," said Itzhak. "I've looked at the convention program, and tomorrow evening is still free, so Ilse can mention it to Mrs. Ny, and perhaps we'll get their confirmation this evening."

"What's the main purpose, Heinrich?"

"My dear Hansel, *that* we'll mull over at the cinema, *n'est-ce pas?*" They continued their meal silently, but they couldn't help looking at everyone who eyed them. Once again, it was hard not to feel paranoid.

They parted at the restaurant entrance.

Heidi did not join them later on Vorontzovskaya Street, and they assumed that Vera had kept her busy until the shops had closed.

After discussing various strategies that might gain them Professor Nevsky's greater confidance, and possession of the information they needed to relay to Max Roth and David Boran, Baruch and Itzhak returned to their hotel at 6:30.

Heidi was not there.

Itzhak was worried. So was Baruch. They paced the room together, looking at each other.

At 7:30, Itzhak went with Baruch to his room.

"It's snowing heavily outside," Baruch said as they entered, and walked over to a table.

He picked up a pad and pencil.

He wrote, "Should we call Professor Ny?"

Baruch wrote; "Wait at least another hour."

"Agreed," wrote Itzhak, and added, "But if there's no sign of her then, and if Ny or Mrs. Ny knows nothing, do I signal Tel-Aviv via the Moscow Cell?"

Baruch wrote: "I think not. Only when all the facts of the emergency are clear to us—if there is an emergency."

"OK," Itzhak wrote. "Let's hope there isn't."

Then he made a great stomping noise over to the window, and said, "It certainly is snowing out there. Come to my room, Fritz, and let's have a drink. I could do with one."

They looked at each other. Their silence was much stronger than words.

Meanwhile, Heidi was trying to cope with one of the most difficult challenges of her career as an SB agent.

She had met Vera Nevsky punctually at three o'clock, as agreed.

For the first few moments together, Heidi hadn't noticed anything strange in her new friend's behavior, probably because Vera was making a conscious effort to appear calm.

Before allowing her to leave for her meeting with Ilse Schuehler, Nevsky had a long and serious conversation with his wife. He had impressed upon her the importance of satisfying two needs, and serving two masters simultaneously.

"You must show your loyalty to the State, and yet not jeopardize people's safety unnecessarily. The State machinery, with it's bureaucratic rules and codes, is naturally impersonal and—as a result—very callous. All legal machinery is, my dear Vera. By coincidence, we may, in this case, use our own judgment about when to set this machinery in motion. Let's use this rare opportunity wisely—though firmly."

Vera had felt unhappy during Nevsky's explanation. It was too cool and scientific, she reflected. As if he were discussing one of his tedious laboratory experiments.

"But more likely than not, it's all a misunderstanding, Iliya. How can I ask Ilse without hurting her feelings?"

The professor shrugged. "If, as you say, it's merely a misunderstanding and they are innocent, it means they are also loyal friends of Russia. And, as such, they'll understand. If not—if Staniev is right, then this is a most serious matter, to be dealt with by the authorities responsible for our national security."

"Then tell me, please," Vera had said in her most sincere manner, "What are your own personal feelings? Your intuition, which is unusually better than any woman's—what does it tell you? Does Ilse, or even her husband, Heinrich, look like a traitor—a spy?"

Nevsky had smiled and kissed her carefully on the forehead, so as not to disarrange her hair.

"You'd be angry with me if I told you your question is childish. So just let me say that it's very kind. It's a lovely reflection of your purity and innocence." He smiled at her. "But, my dearest, it completely disregards the stern realities of our devious world, and human deception. The best spies, and enemy agents, are also the best actors. It is their profession. Do not ask me to try and guess what goes on behind their greasepaint."

The event that had given rise to this conversation was an unexpected phone call, received by the professor early in the morning.

The caller had been his onetime friend from Leipzig, Dr. Staniev, who had himself just arrived at the convention.

Nevsky had met Staniev for breakfast and laughingly told him more about the previous night's meeting with the two young scientists coming from the same school as his. He had told Staniev of their visit to the Explosion, and of the quantity of vodka he had drunk.

"I think they were rather amazed that I could put it away like I did," he said.

Staniev said nothing.

Dr. Staniev had mentioned on the telephone that he had not met or heard of two doctors of pharmacology with the names of either Hansel or Schuehler.

Nevsky had assured Staniev that there could be no mistake, and stressed how impressed he had been with their charm and obviously superior intelligence. He had also mentioned Ilse Schuehler, but this information too, had met with Staniev's ignorance of such a person.

"Really! It's all rather curious." he said at breakfast. His voice was dry. "I pride myself on knowing our graduates personally. Of course, I may be mistaken—but of a Heinrich and Ilse Schuehler, or a Fritz Hansel from our faculty—no. I'm afraid I've never heard of them."

Professor Nevsky stared at him, and shook his head slowly.

"I agree, it's rather strange—one might even say, suspicious," Nevsky said. "Naturally, I consider it my duty to look into the matter at once."

They had left it at that, and Nevsky had later had his talk with Vera . . . before she set out on her tour with Ilse Schuehler.

First, Vera had taken Heidi to nearby Red Square, and pointed out the statue of Maxim Gorki—glancing at her curiously, as if measuring her reaction to the famous view of the vast expanse bordered by the red-brown wall of the Kremlin, behind which the cupolas and spires formed a fairyland silhouette in their gleaming snowy whiteness.

Then they had walked up part of stately Gorki Street into one of the city's less crowded shopping districts.

"It's all very beautiful," Heidi said, happy that she was able to be sincere.

"Then this is your first time in Moscow, Ilse?"

Heidi looked at her.

"Oh, yes. I told you so last night, remember?"

It was Vera's turn to look at Heidi.

"So you did. I must have forgotten. Also, your husband and Herr Hansel, have they never visited here before?"

Already, Heidi was getting tense inside.

"No, Vera. And they, too, are most impressed."

"Strange. Very strange in a way. Leipzig is so near, nowadays. Iliya and I have been to Berlin several times."

Now Heidi was definitely on the defensive.

"Heinrich only received his doctorate two years ago. Your husband already had his when you were married, didn't he?"

"Yes."

"You can imagine what men are like when they work on their theses. I don't think we got beyond the suburbs until last year."

Vera smiled. It was genuine.

"Yes, I do understand that." What *was* the woman getting at. Heidi stole a look at Vera's face. But she caught no expression whatever. The lips were smiling, the eyes pleasant.

Heidi relaxed a bit.

For the next hour or two the conversation remained wholly concerned with clothing.

They inspected, and tried on, numerous things but found little to really interest them.

Vera tried to urge Heidi to purchase a winter coat, but Heidi confessed that she couldn't afford such an extravagance.

Vera looked at Heidi attentively as she said, "I don't mean to be rude but how much do young scientists earn in Leipzig?"

The question did not relieve Heidi's anxiety. However, that particular piece of information had been included in their indoctrination. She told Vera.

"Really!" the Russian woman said. "That isn't much." She sighed, "But I suppose an older and more established scientist like Dr. Staniev must be getting much more."

"Well, yes, Vera, but maybe his Russian background has something to do with it, too," Heidi ventured.

Vera laughed, but Heidi thought she detected something in the laughter that wasn't real. The Russian woman said, "It's nice to hear we form an élite—in East Germany at least."

Heidi tightened her lips, and hoped it didn't show. Her stomach felt like a drumskin again. I'm still giving the right answers she thought, but this woman sure is asking a lot of questions—and they're not connected with our shopping, either.

Half an hour later, the two women sat in the quaint Georgian restaurant enjoying a spicy *shishlik* with a sesame seed-oil salad, another specialty of the house.

It was delicious, but Heidi noticed that Vera hardly touched her food. Actually, the Russian woman's mind was too preoccupied with the unpleasant mission she had been charged with by her husband. If Ilse and her companions were spies, how could she hope to outwit even one of them. If not, she was certainly on the point of making a fool of herself.

"We had such a wonderful time last night, Vera. It's made Heinrich and myself and also Fritz anxious to see you as often as possible while we're here."

"Thank you, Ilse. We're glad you enjoyed it. Iliya is a special patron of the Explosion, and he asked me to tell you he hopes to see you all very soon."

Heidi smiled, "That's so good to hear, Vera. I've been wanting to ask you this for the past two hours. Heinrich and Fritz have ordered a table for dinner tomorrow night at a restaurant which looks very pleasant. They expect me to succeed in persuading you and the professor to join us again—even if just for an hour."

Heidi couldn't help noticing that the Russian woman stiffened. But on the other hand, her smile was charmingly unforced.

"That was kind of them, Ilse, and I can only promise you that I shall do my best to get Iliya to come. Of course, you know how busy he is with the convention."

Vera paused for a moment, then continued, "Perhaps it would be best if you talked with him yourself.

The other woman always has a better chance." She smiled.

Heidi did not foresee the trap and replied, "Of course. Should I call your husband now?"

"No, no. It will not be necessary. I don't even know where Iliya will be before seven o'clock tonight. So here's what we'll do. We'll finish our shopping by six-thirty and join Iliya at the university canteen at seven. That was, anyway, what we arranged before I came to meet you."

Heidi hesitated. She would have to let either Itzhak or Baruch know, but she could see no reason for objecting to Vera's suggestion. It might be the easiest way of deepening their relationship with the Nevskys. And that was vitally important.

"That sounds good. But are you sure your husband will want me to disturb him again so soon?"

"I'll let you in on a secret, Ilse. Iliya actually asked me to bring you along to the university this evening. In fact, I think I ought to be jealous."

They both laughed, and Heidi said, "I'll have to call Heinrich. I told him I'd be back at six-thirty."

She looked at her wristwatch. It was just after 5:30. They had had their lunch very late, but both of them wanted to get most of the shopping and sightseeing done during the least busy hours. Heidi knew she could not call Itzhak at the cinema, and that Itzhak and Baruch would wait for her there until six.

"Please . . . Come with me." Vera paused. "I'll show you where the telephones are. Then I'll call and leave a message for Iliya at the university."

Heidi was getting very nervous.

"I'm afraid Heinrich isn't at the hotel right now. I'd better call after six-thirty."

"No, Ilse. I'm afraid that will be just when we have to take the Metro back to Komsomolskaya, so just call your husband from the university when we get there."

Heidi could think of no reasonable excuse to insist on calling earlier, though this would have given her the chance of talking with Itzhak from the privacy of a phone booth.

. . . 11

The heavy traffic on the Underground, and the snow outside—which had begun to turn into a small blizzard—delayed the two women. By the time they reached the canteen, it was ten minutes past seven. Professor Nevsky was waiting for them.

The strategy of bringing Ilse Schuehler along without allowing her to return to the Hotel Berlin, or to consult with either of the two men, had constituted the main part of his instructions to Vera, and Nevsky was truly pleased with her for carrying out her mission with such obvious success.

Heidi noticed that there were three telephones available, but they were not inside a booth, or even behind a screen. They were, therefore, quite useless, from her point of view.

"My dear Frau Schuehler!" Nevsky received her with a show of slightly exaggerated delight. "How good of you to come. How was your shopping?" He took Vera by her arm, and led them both to a vacant booth.

There were few people in the canteen.

"I bought very little," Vera replied. "As you can see by the small number and size of my packages."

"And I was quite happy window-shopping," said Heidi.

They ordered tea and Scandinavian-style open sandwiches. Professor Nevsky allowed the conversation to drift along aimlessly for five minutes or so, and then he broached the subject that formed the reason for this apparently casual meeting.

He might have thought he was an actor, but Heidi knew better. She realized what he was doing.

"By the way, Dr. Staniev gave me a call this morning." The professor scrutinized Heidi's face for her reaction, and she felt it. She managed to control herself perfectly, though Nevsky's eyes were schooled.

"Staniev?" For a moment she had made an effort to recall the name, which she had heard for the first time twenty-four hours before.

"Yes. One of your husband and Herr Hansel's professors at Leipzig University."

"Of course." She was tense again. Tense all over. "Now I remember. You see, I've never met him personally, though Heinrich has mentioned his name to me from time to time." Heidi hoped she had not given herself away already. Also, that she was adopting the safest approach possible. Nevsky's next words however, convinced her otherwise.

"Did he? Well, both Heinrich and Fritz seemed rather certain they knew Staniev well when I asked them yesterday. And in view of that, I naturally mentioned your names to him this morning."

The professor paused significantly. He looked straight into Heidi's eyes with slightly lowered lids—perhaps expecting some immediate and innocent explanation.

"In fact, my dear Frau Schuehler, Dr. Staniev insists he has never come across the names Hansel and Schuehler during his entire career at Leipzig. Strange . . . don't you think?"

Heidi quickly decided that her only feasible strategy was to stall for time, and somehow get a message to Itzhak and Baruch.

She could only pray they had not already been picked up for questioning by the Militia, or even KGB. "I'm sure there must be some misunderstanding, some simple explanation. Of course, I'll ask Heinrich the moment I get back to the hotel."

"Please do that, Ilse. Meanwhile, I expect Staniev will be contacting him, and asking the same questions."

For the first time, Vera interposed. "Look, Iliya why don't you try to get the explanation yourself—before Staniev gets more involved.

In fact, the professor had assured Staniev that he would try to find out the reasons behind the apparent masquerade, and let him know this evening.

Staniev had agreed to desist from taking official steps until he had heard from Nevsky. But, of course, there could be no assurance that he wouldn't have second thoughts, and renege on their agreement.

"Please let me call my husband. I am sure he must he back at the hotel by now," Heidi had decided that anything was better than wasting more time.

It became quite clear the professor would not give. her a chance to speak with the hotel from a phone where he could not overhear her.

She was becoming more and more wise to the manner in which he was working.

"Good, Ilse. We'll walk over to the telephone together. I'm sure you understand. I'm not distrustful by nature—Vera will vouch for that—but until I know what to tell Staniev, I simply dare not take any risks, even with someone so charming as you."

There was nothing else to be done.

They walked across the canteen—Nevsky, one step behind Heidi, and remaining within arm's reach. She dialed the number of the hotel.

Itzhak was not in his room.

Heidi asked the operator to try a second time. Then she asked to have the call put through to Baruch's room.

But, there, also, the call went unanswered.

Professor Nevsky, who had watched her endeavors to reach her husband and friend and judged them to be sincere, shrugged his shoulders, and said:

"My dear Ilse, I must simply ask you to come home with us, and continue your efforts to contact your husband from there. You're not my prisoner. I have no right to force you, but if you refuse, I have no other recourse than to put the matter into the hands of the Militia, who will ask you all the relevant questions in the presence of Dr. Staniev. The choice remains in your hands."

There was a rigid look on his face now. Heidi did not doubt what he said.

She knew she could not bluff her way out of the impasse. She agreed to accompany them to their Gorkova Prospekt apartment.

It was 7:35 p.m.

She had called one minute after Itzhak and Baruch had left Baruch's room to get a drink in Itzhak's. On their way along the hallway, Itzhak had remembered that the only bottle in his room was almost empty, and they had decided to go down to the basement bar by the short servant's stairway without bothering to wait for the elevator. They were convinced that a few minutes away from their rooms could not matter. Of course, they kept their room keys in their pockets, and the desk clerk had not been asked by Heidi to page them in the bar.

Heidi's only immediate choice was to remain Professor Iliya Petrovitch Nevsky's voluntary hostage, until the two men could be contacted.

She also decided on remaining behind, and covering for them as long as possible, in the event of their escape. This was neither a gesture of bravado or helpless despair.

Heidi had long ago concluded that men like Itzhak and Baruch were indispensable to Security Branch. She had no such illusion about herself, and had made up her mind that, as a last resort anytime, she would offer herself as a sacrifice—if this would give them that extra hour or two in which to make good a getaway.

When Itzhak and Baruch entered the basement bar of the Hotel Berlin, a tall, baldheaded man in his late fifties stood in a telephone booth across the street and dialed Professor Nevsky's number.

He dialed twice, and got a busy signal.

A notoriously impatient man, Dr. Staniev decided to dial the hotel, whose entrance he could see through the glass door of the booth.

The operator received the second calls for either Herr Schuehler or Herr Hansel within five minutes.

This time, however, the person calling, requested that they be paged in the foyer, restaurant, and bar.

As a result, they were located.

Itzhak went to the phone hoping the call was from Heidi. He was excited. Baruch followed close behind and tried to listen in by putting his head near the receiver.

Dr. Staniev had thought a lot all that day, about a certain Herr Hansel and a certain Herr Schuehler. They sounded fake. He had no intention of allowing his good name to get mixed up with monkey business, possibly even with espionage. Only out of friendship for Iliya Petrovitch Nevsky had he agreed to wait until evening before taking decisive action. He had tried to call Nevsky several times at home and at the university, but either the professor had been out or the line was busy.

In the meantime, the birds might fly the coop. Why did they claim to know him? They had never been in his classes, or fellow faculty members.

To that, Staniev could swear.

Whatever happened, he must either report the matter before the day was out, or verify their identity on his own.

Staniev had finally decided that he would keep trying to get hold of Nevsky until early evening. Failing, he would take a look at his two supposed fellow scientists before sounding the alarm.

This, he felt certain, could be done at ease inside their hotel.

When Itzhak picked up the receiver, Staniev did not identify himself, but asked: "Is this Herr Hansel, or Herr Schuehler speaking?"

"It is Heinrich Schuehler."

"Good. You're in the hotel bar, I believe?"

"Yes."

"Good, Herr Schuehler. It's rather important that I speak both to you and Herr Hansel. I shall be over in about fifteen minutes."

Itzhak and Baruch had no intention of making a run for it. Not with Heidi's whereabouts unknown. The caller, who had failed to identify himself over the phone, might well be one of their own Security Branch undercover men—or Russian collaborator.

The small hotel bar was almost empty when the tall stranger who entered a quarter of an hour later walked straight up to them with the confidence of an old acquaintance.

"I'm a friend of Professor Iliya Petrovitch Nevsky," said Staniev. "Which of you is Herr Schuehler?"

Itzhak introduced himself.

"Your wife is also here—upstairs in her room, perhaps?"

"No, she is out—Herr . . . ?"

"I'll tell you my name in a moment. You have my promise. But first I shall very quietly promise you something else." This man had an ominous but somewhat theatrical inclination as he continued. "When I tell you who I am, you may be surprised. You may be afraid. Perhaps you will decide to get up and run. I very strongly advise you against such a foolish action. We are in central Moscow. There are at least four Militia stations within a stone's throw of this hotel. You would not get far, I assure you. And if you're armed, it would be childish on your part to shoot me." He shrugged and spread his hands. "Why commit suicide? I'm not yet threatening you with anything. Perhaps the professor misunderstood and it's all a big mistake."

Then the man paused, obviously intent on building up the tension he felt sure he had already created.

"Now, I'll tell you who I am." He hesitated, watching them, his eyes turning from one to another. "And if by chance you do not wish to believe me, I shall be only too happy to accompany you to the nearest Militia station in order to identify myself." Again he hesitated. There was a change in the texture of his voice. "I am Dr. Igor Alexandrevitch Staniev, for the past twelve years lecturing at Leipzig University." He paused again, waiting, expecting a reaction.

But there was none. Neither man batted an eyelash. Security Branch training had trained them well.

"And who, gentlemen, are you?"

By mutual agreement, arrived at with a single glance, Itzhak answered for them both.

"What will you say—or do—if we simply refuse to tell you?"

"Exactly what I'll do if you attempt to walk out of here—without my consent." The last three words were harsh.

"Well, it is all very strange and meaningless to me—and to my friend here, I assure you," said Itzhak. "You're obviously neither Militia nor KGB. Yet, with the convention opening tomorrow, I admit a ridiculous and time-consuming investigation would be highly inconvenient. We shall probably launch an official complaint against you when the convention is over. But for the moment . . ."

Itzhak placed his East German passport, Communist Party membership card, and official invitation to the convention on the bar table in front of Staniev.

Baruch followed suit. Staniev studied the documents very closely, paying particular attention to the Party card.

Instinctively, they realized they had gained an advantage over the scientist.

Dr. Staniev had been sure he was confronting a gang of criminals or spies. Now, suddenly he found himself with a very difficult decision to make.

Should he denounce these men forthwith, in defiance of all the documentation before him? Or had he better take it easy and make sure of the ground he stood on? If he chose the first course, he risked becoming a laughing stock, a stupid busybody who claimed to be more perspicacious than a dozen Militia and KGB men, passport and immigration officials, and other experts specially trained for their jobs.

"Assuming, then, that these documents are in good order and belong to you, would you kindly explain to me why you told Professor Nevsky that you are representatives of my university, and why you claim to know me personally?"

Baruch had paid special attention to the word

"kindly." He felt he knew a good gambit that might push Staniev further off-balance.

"How well do you really know Professor Nevsky?" asked Baruch.

Staniev seemed to be taken aback. "We spent years together doing undergraduate work. Of course, my work in Leipzig these past years has kept us apart for long periods."

"Then perhaps you're not aware that the good professor drinks rather heavily, though not regularly—which only enhances the effects of alcohol. Last night we were happy to present him with two duty-free bottles of fine American whiskey. He also went out with us to a night club, and drank heavily. Although he didn't show it, all that alcohol was bound to effect him in some way. I believe he finished one whole bottle while we chatted about various places in Germany—including Leipzig—as well as our work. That hardly makes him a reliable witness to anything we might, or might not, have said, does it?"

Staniev's voice was lower now. "No, Herr Hansel, I admit it doesn't. However, this would still not explain your presence here at the Moscow Scientific Research Convention."

"Point by point, Dr. Staniev," Baruch continued, hoping to impress their accuser with this common, methodical analysis. "One, my friend and I never claimed to have met you—though of course, as scientists born in Leipzig, we followed some of your work in pharmacology. But to come back to last night: It was Nevsky who mentioned you several times and, indeed, asked whether we knew you. Apparently, our negative reply was lost in his alcoholic haze.

"Point two. We never claimed to be post-graduates at Leipzig, but told Nevsky clearly that it was Heidelberg, and that our invitations to the convention were sent by Moscow to Leipzig as a result of one of those forgivable mixups that always happen when hundreds of guests are invited from many countries. We've already received the apology of the organizing committee, and their reasonable explanation that our place of birth—

Leipzig—had inadvertently been confused with our place of work—Heidelberg."

Baruch leaned back with an air of self-assurance and lit a cigarette. There was a certain complacency about his style. Itzhak smiled indulgently at Staniev, who was now fidgeting in his chair and beginning to betray overt symptoms of discomfort.

Had they really succeeded in persuading him that he was making an ass of himself?

"Gentlemen," he said after some time. "I hope you're fair-minded enough to grant that I had every sound reason for suspecting you. Bonafide loyal citizens and decent Communists," he half turned to Itzhak, "are duty bound to have the security of the Democratic German Republic and the Soviet Union at heart. Therefore, even if I have been completely mistaken, I can't regret my action here."

He rose, and bowed stiffly with the upper part of his back and neck, as if his spinal column were endowed with a special hinge. The anachronism of his bow, combined with Staniev's speech, would have amused the Israelis more had his manners not sprung from a situation that ten minutes earlier had appeared very bleak indeed.

They parted, with no time wasted on amiability.

Itzhak looked at his watch. It was already eight-thirty. There was no message at the desk from Frau Schuehler. By common consent, they decided to defy the extreme cold outside and take a brisk walk around the block. They did not want to be away from the hotel—and a possible phone call from Heidi—for very long.

And they had to talk. As soon as they were out in the street, wrapped in their warmest clothes, Itzhak commenced:

"Thanks man, you did a good job." He gave a short laugh. "I had just about run dry, believe me. There were no more ideas. But let's not fool ourselves. Staniev hasn't given up. He'll be on the phone to Heidelberg University first thing tomorrow morning, if he doesn't call tonight." He paused. "On the other hand, we can be pretty sure he won't call Nevsky. What would he say to him? 'Tell me, dear Iliya Petrovitch, is it true you were drunk last night?' So we are left with two problems. One, how to find Heidi. And two, how, or if, to go underground."

Baruch was slapping his arms together for warmth. "We have to cope with both these problems together. We can't wait long. As you say, Staniev might have the KGB on our tails before the night's out, and God knows what's happening to Heidi. It looks as though we'll have to kiss our invitations to the convention good-bye in any case, so let's get the hell out of that hotel and contact the Cell. I know that Roth and Boran will hate what we're doing. Those Cells in the Red countries are their holy cows, and by going underground here in Moscow, we risk blowing their cover as well as our own."

"And it's taken Tel-Aviv ten years to build the Moscow Cell up to what it is today, Baruch. We're sticking, not only our own necks out, but also the necks of half a dozen good men. Still, I admit I don't see a better solution. At least, we can go on looking for Heidi, and working on the Mokhavaya Street mission at the same time."

He didn't tell Baruch what he was feeling.

"Yes," said Baruch. "Until we've found her—or she's found us."

. . . 12

At Professor Nevsky's apartment on Gorkova Prospekt, Heidi had phoned a few minutes before eight, but there was again no answer.

Vera Nevsky had said very little, making tea, and putting a plate of homemade cakes on the table. No one seemed inclined to eat.

The professor remained kind but firm in his manner toward Heidi. Unlike Staniev, he did not interrogate his "prisoner." Somehow, he could not visualize Ilse Schuehler in the role of a spy or saboteur. More likely than not, he told himself, she had become innocently involved in dirty business that she knew nothing about.

Vera would not easily forgive him, were he to hurt Ilse unjustly.

Heidi's antennae had begun to pick up the favorable vibrations of the improved atmosphere.

Nevsky lowered his voice. "Tell me honestly, dear," he said for the fifth time, merely asking the question in different ways. "Haven't you some idea of what they're up to? Why are they here in Moscow?"

Heidi had begun to wonder whether the time hadn't come for her to play her cards differently.

With each minute that passed, Professor Nevsky, and Vera, appeared to her more and more to be friendly people who, though they could never be expected to act against the safety and welfare of their own country, would also not take part in the Arab war against Israel.

Now she spoke aloud. "What can I say, Professor Nevsky? We've known each other for less than two days. You've been very kind, and Vera seems like an old friend. Wouldn't it be best to forget us, to let me go, if I give you my solemn word that we're not here to undertake any action that may damage your country?"

"Iliya and I both pride ourselves on our ability to judge character, don't we, darling?" said Vera.

"Yes, dear, we do," Nevsky replied.

Vera turned to Heidi and continued. "And we judge you, yes, and also your husband and Herr Hansel to be decent people." She paused and shook her head. "Iliya is in a difficult position because of Staniev. He can't just say to him: 'Well, Staniev, these young scientists from your university probably just forgot they had never really met you. And as for your never having known them—perhaps it's *your* mistake. You're getting old, Staniev!' There has to be either a good answer for Staniev, or a very good reason why Iliya should accept the great risk of protecting you."

The professor smiled. "You said that perfectly, my dear," he said. He picked up Vera's slender hand and kissed it. "We scientists are famous for our thirst for truth. It is a subject often joked about. We can't function in twilight. We abhore uncertainty, and reject equivocation. These are rules by which I have tried to live all my adult life—not only as a scientist but also as a human being: a decent, human being among my fellow people. I've tried never to accuse or judge without a knowledge of all the facts, but neither can I attempt to understand—or help—while I remain ignorant."

Vera turned to Heidi. "If you're in trouble Ilse, please tell us. Please! Trust us."

Nevsky continued: "If you need help, you must first help yourself by being honest with us. I should add—though this must sound cruel—that you need not accuse yourself of breaking vows or promises you may have made, because your only alternative is having the authorities extract the truth ruthlessly. I can tell you that honestly. I can make you no promises, Ilse, but the only way you can persuade us to help you is to tell us the truth."

It was not a decision to be taken lightly by Heidi.

Fundamentally, it ran counter to all the principles of security training.

One of the primary SB taboos was, of course, the unauthorized breaking of cover—especially in hostile territory and at the height of an operation involving other agents. Involving, in this case, an entire Security Branch Cell.

Heidi searched within herself to discover the best thing to do.

She found no unnatural fear for her personal safety. Her continued silence would no longer protect Itzhak and Baruch—not since Staniev had entered the picture.

Under the present circumstances, which she had no means of altering, all undercover efforts to further their mission were hamstrung.

They could, in any case, no longer attend the convention, or get into the Mokhavaya Street laboratories.

"I'll try to let you help us," she said solemnly. "Again, I want to assure you that we're not spies sent to harm the Soviet Union. We're also convinced that you are being used—though ignorant of the fact—for an evil and murderous purpose. You have said many wise things, Professor. And one of these was this: that as a scientist and decent human being, you felt unable to function in the dark, that knowledge of the facts was, for you, like water to a thirsty man."

She stopped briefly, trying to dramatize her discourse, turning toward Vera and taking one of her hands.

"And yet we believe that is exactly what has happened to you without your knowledge. Please don't be shocked at my audacity. Hear me out. and then judge me—in accordance with the very principles you've just set forth.

"We know the nature of your work, and respect your conviction that it is wholly concerned with the security of your country. Throughout the world, nations are stockpiling conventional and unconventional weapons and materials of war, hoping by this means to discourage enemy attack—to avert war. Honorable men like you have agreed to lend their knowledge and skills to the governments of their homelands. We deeply respect this, but destructive forces alien to your country are about to use the results of your work against people who are not your enemy."

Professor Nevsky had leaned forward and was listening intently. Vera looked at him expectantly.

"Well, Ilse, I must say you're an excellent advocate for your cause, whatever that may be. You've spoken of principles with which I agree. I accept your assurance that neither you, Heinrich, nor Hansel is engaged in subversive activities against the USSR." He paused as though to give emphasis to his words. "And I hope that you, too, do not question my sincerity in claiming to know absolutely nothing of what you have been hinting at. My dear Ilse—you have used the personal pronoun 'we' so many times, without defining who you are. Don't you think the time has come to do so?"

Vera pressed Heidi's hand, and added, "Please, Ilse, believe in my husband. Tell us who you really are."

Heidi gave them a succinct outline of most of the facts, omitting to mention Security Branch as such, but making their mission appear in the light of "private enterprise."

Neither did she mention the existence of an Israeli Underground Cell in Moscow. She dwelled upon the facts of the cholera outbreak, thus giving Professor Nevsky convincing evidence of its unnatural cause. She told him of the suffering, of the people who had died. She told him of Benjamin Schneider.

She lent all the urgency she possibly could to their present mission which, she said, had one aim alone: to prevent the germs from being used again in the Israeli water system.

She asked Nevsky and Vera not, at that moment, to press her into revealing their true names.

Professor Nevsky had been pacing back and forth as she talked. Now he stopped in front of her. His dark features were pale.

"Fantastic!" he exclaimed. "Unbelievable if true. I must have proof. What you have said is not enough. I need proof—irrefutable proof."

He paused and stared at her. "I believe in your sincerity Ilse. You're convinced that everything your superiors in Israel have told you is true. But that alone cannot convince me. But the moment you succeed in bringing me adequate evidence, you will have my personal support. I don't think the Jews in Israel are doing everything right, or acting in their own best interests by permitting the growth of theocratic authority, but heaven forbid that we here in Russia should lend active support to Arab terrorism and murderers."

Vera smiled at Heidi, a blush of excitement on the high cheekbones of her beautiful face, which only emphasized her natural paleness. "You see, my dear, your openness with Iliya has had the very best result. He will be fair and give you every chance to produce the evidence he needs."

Heidi nodded. "Thank you. I put my trust in you both, and hope I will fully justify yours." She paused, then said, "Now I think I'd better try the phone again."

Heidi attempted to reach Itzhak or Baruch at the hotel. There was still no answer in either room.

She left the phone feeling dismay, but made every effort to hide it.

"You have my pledge, Iliya and Vera, that I'll keep in constant contact with you. But now I've got to go and try to find the others."

"Go. And good luck!" said Nevsky.

"I'll be at home all day tomorrow," Vera added. "So you can get me anytime." She turned to the professor. "What should I say to Staniev, if he calls when you're out?"

The professor mused.

"Since he hasn't called again yet, maybe he's waiting for the convention opening tomorrow. Just tell him I've investigated Schuehler and Hansel, and that I'll fill him in sometime during the day."

The Professor took Heidi to the nearby Metro station. As they said good-bye, Professor Nevsky pressed her hand.

. . . 13

Itzhak and Baruch had been walking the streets near the Hotel Berlin. They were cold to the marrow, and wondering still what to do. They had reached the hotel entrance again.

Itzhak was terribly worried about Heidi.

Suddenly Baruch exclaimed, "Look!" He pointed down the street where the rapidly approaching figure of Heidi was heading toward them.

Itzhak only with difficulty refrained from joyfully shouting her real name.

She ran toward them.

Wordlessly, Itzhak took her into his arms, and Baruch was obliged to bide his time until their embrace had ended. "I never want to let go of you again," said Itzhak.

"I feel the same way," said Heidi.

Baruch suggested they first go to their rooms to prepare for their "exodus." Heidi nodded.

Inside their rooms, they put on layer after layer of underwear and sweaters, hoping the night clerk downstairs would not notice their sudden gain in weight.

Carrying nothing in their hands besides Heidi's largest handbag, and the same "James Bond" cases which Itzhak and Baruch had already carried in and out of the hotel, they departed. Only when they were several blocks away from the hotel did they hail a taxi, asking the driver to take them to Vorontzovskaya Street.

People were just entering the cinema for the last show, and they had decided it would be quite safe and unobtrusive for them to stop for a brief strategy meeting—and possibly to make the necessary phone calls to Security Branch contacts in the city.

". . . and so I spilled the beans. I told them almost everything," Heidi said. "Vera was very nice. They both were. But the professor is still doubtful, I'm afraid. I didn't tell them our real names."

Then Itzhak very briefly filled her in on their encounter with Dr. Staniev, and the need for their disappearance.

As soon as Itzhak finished, Heidi made a phone call to the Nevskys and, without identifying herself, told them in simple words, that Dr. Staniev would certainly not call during the next few hours, but that they must expect him to initiate an official hue by the following afternoon at the latest.

Then Itzhak made a call.

"Schuehler here. Ilse and Fritz send their regards. We are all at the . . . cinema on Vorontzovskaya Street. The weather is very bad. Please pick us up without delay."

"Right. In twenty minutes."

"*Spassivo.*"

Itzhak put the receiver down, and they went out into the street.

It had not been snowing when they arrived, but now the wind drove heavy flakes into their faces.

While they waited, Baruch and Itzhak reassured Heidi about her actions.

She had been inclined to castigate herself, and to invite their rebuke for breaking their cover, but they stressed that, for all intents and purposes, their cover was already blown by Staniev, and by their disappearance from the Hotel Berlin—which would be discovered by the cleaning woman in the morning.

They were also certain the KGB would be onto them. Their rooms would be searched. The KGB would question the Nevskys. The Israelis mourned this fact, but there was nothing they could do about it. They thought of warning Professor Nevsky, but knew it would do no good.

"The Schuehlers and their associate, Hansel, have

ceased to exist," Itzhak said. "For the moment, we're nameless, but I expect Roth and Boran will soon have us back in circulation somehow."

His lighthearted optimism did not fool Baruch. He could easily see that Itzhak was worried.

Baruch said, "Farewell, dark eyes, dark hair. I only hope our next ID isn't going to involve a crash course in one of the Chinese dialects of the People's Republic."

"Thanks for your humor—if it's meant to cheer me up," Heidi said. "But in snowstorms like this, I'd rather get instructions in Arctic survival techniques."

She was shivering, and hugging herself.

A small Jiguli sedan drew up, its driver pushing the door open from the inside, and asking in a muffled voice:

"Schuehler? Hansel?"

"Yes."

"Get in. Quick!"

They got in.

The little car made a U-turn.

There was no conversation.

The driver asked only whether they were all in good physical shape.

Whoever was responsible for the Cell had assumed that one or more of them was ill or wounded—perhaps the most likely reason he could think of for their abrupt, unexpected call.

The Cell's task was primarily to feed information back to Israel regarding Russian arms supplied to Egypt and Syria, mutual visits by statesmen, generals and military advisors, and new secret agreements or disagreements between the Kremlin and Arab governments, or differences of opinion between various factions fighting for supremecy inside the Kremlin itself—insofar as they concerned the Middle East conflict.

It had all the resources of a first-rate overseas intelligence headquarters at its disposal—but only to be used for prima-facie espionage.

Such Cells required years to organize. And to blow

its cover would be considered a cardinal sin by Israeli leadership.

The driver suddenly turned his head and asked, "How is Max? Still suffering from dandruff?"

His three passengers forgave the driver his ill-cloaked ID security probe.

"His bald head shines as usual," Itzhak said, and laughed.

Sometime later, the driver asked, "What was playing at Mograbi Cinema last week?"

This time Heidi—the only regular cinema fan among them—came to the rescue.

"*Live and Let Die*—James Bond."

"Are the coffee and cake at the Ibn Gabriol Roval still good?" the driver asked, more jokingly now—referring to one of Tel-Aviv's most famous cafes, which had unexpectedly closed a few weeks before.

"*Roval-yok,* as the Turks would say," said Baruch, and the driver's impromptu check of their ID seemed to have come to a satisfactory conclusion.

The Jiguli sedan was taking them into a district of narrow roads and quaint, old-fashioned apartment houses, dating back to the '20s and '30s.

It was quite dark. Snow was falling heavily. The streets were deep in it. Traffic was surprisingly heavy.

They stopped outside a four-story tenement house with a sign, just legible in the dim light of the street lamp: KURUMALISKAYA STREET NO. 99.

A narrow dark alley beside the building led them to a back yard, just large enough to hold two small cars and their tiny Jiguli.

"We get out here," the driver said. "Come with me."

They followed him down another very narrow alley—so narrow, in fact, that their shoulders brushed the sides of the buildings that hemmed it in.

A door opened.

"Inside, and up those stairs."

They went inside and began to climb a dingy staircase. There was only one light—at the top—and that was shielded.

The building was icy. The driver followed them.

At the top of the stairway, under the dim bulb, there was a door.

The driver knocked twice.

The door was opened by a tall dark man.

The driver said, "Here they are."

The driver looked at the Israelis, then back at the man in the doorway.

"They're all right," said the driver.

"Then go."

The driver turned, walked down the stairway, and left.

"Come in," the man at the door said.

Itzhak, Heidi, and Baruch followed him into the room.

There were three men inside. One was an obvious Israeli.

He stood up and looked at them with dark eyes that were quite steady. His mouth was broad and turned up at the corners. "Well."

Baruch, Itzhak, and Heidi gave the three Cell members an outline of the events that had led up to their presence.

The Israeli was the Cell leader. He wanted to know everything about Dr. Staniev—at which hotel he was staying, whether he had a family in Moscow.

Itzhak was unable to tell him. And it was apparent that the information Itzhak was able to supply about Professor Nevsky and his work was not news.

"OK," the Cell leader said, when Itzak concluded. "I think you did about the only thing you could. You weren't exactly left with much of a choice. Of course, I don't know what reaction there will be in Israel. Meantime, the three of you have to stay here." He shrugged and spread his hands. He was wearing a dark turtleneck sweater and tight pants. "For all we know, Staniev might already have called Heidelberg, and Militia may be on the lookout for you in the streets. We'll have to get you a completely new ID, and your appearance must be changed drastically."

"How long will it take?" asked Heidi.

"It's up to Tel-Aviv. We can only be responsible for

the job of protecting you and, if necessary, getting you out of Russia." The man's face tightened. His eyes seemed to grow darker. "Damn it all, that's going to be tough. But I think we can manage it . . . But only if Tel-Aviv is authorized to decide for or against the continuation of your mission."

"But remember," said Baruch, "for God's sake: the mission has a time limit. SUW is in a flap about this cholera threat." Baruch spoke with heat.

"True," Itzhak said. "But we're no longer limited to the convention. Our contact with Nevsky is established. Thanks to Heidi, we'll have him firmly on our side as soon as we can show him proof that those germs are destined for shipment to the Arabs."

The Cell leader nodded. "We'll include that subject in our message to Tel-Aviv. The moment I have photostatic evidence showing that PFLP, Al Fatah, or any group has been promised these containers by Moscow, I'll see that Nevsky gets it. But how long it's going to take won't depend on us."

For the first time, one of the other Cell members contributed to the conversation.

"Let's prepare the message. Our guests had better settle down. They'll have to figure out how to sleep. This isn't the Hotel Berlin, but it's a hell of a lot better than a cell in Lubyanka Prison."

Heidi wondered.

The two identical rooms at the other side of the narrow hallway had tile stoves, but they could not be used because wood smoke rising from the chimney would be blatant evidence of twenty-four-hour occupation.

There was a battered couch, and a motheaten easy chair in one room, and a three-quarter bed in the other. Baruch resigned himself to the camp bed.

One of the Cell members, a rather plump man in a gray coat and sweater, stood in the doorway. "Tomorrow, there'll be a few blankets," he said. "We really can't walk up with pillows and bedding. And you won't go hungry. I suggest you try to get the oil stove in the kitchen going first thing in the morning. I'll be over with a thermos of coffee. It'll help keep the cold out of your blood."

They thanked him for being so solicitous, wondering about his nationality and background and the reasons behind his decision to work for Security Branch. But they would neither ask him nor even discuss it among themselves.

Undercover agents, under certain circumstances, remained nameless, their ID known only in the very highest quarters.

The Cell leader had already told them how to address or refer to him. He was *"99."*

...14

Max Roth received the urgent message from Security Branch in Moscow at 3:00 a.m. on Saturday, December 9.

Though he was not an orthodox Jew, the Sabbath was his normal day of rest and relaxation devoted to his wife—and grandchildren, of whom he had three, ages one to five.

To be roused out of his bed at 3:00 a.m. on a wet, wintry Saturday was not, therefore, liable to contribute to his joviality, of which there had never been a surplus.

"Get me Dave Boran," he shouted into his bedside phone. "Why should the rest of SB sleep when I can't?"

Five minutes later, both Roth and Colonel David Boran were in their cars, headed for Security Branch Headquarters near Tel-Aviv.

They reached the huge iron gates that opened on the driveway leading to Iceberg Building within thirty seconds of each other, and passed the identification checks at the gate and again at the side entrance. A winding flight of concrete steps led down to the elevator. They descended in it to Roth's office situated some twenty feet below-ground.

The Military and Air Force Intelligence Headquarters occupied bunkers still lower.

That is why it was called Iceberg Building.

"Sit down if you like, Dave," said Roth, as he hopped forth and back on the dusty cement floor. "I'm too damn cold, and I can't be bothered to put down the carpet before the floor's washed."

A Signal Corps sergeant, with immense shoulders and a chin you could have hung a hat on, entered and handed Roth a lengthy decoded message.

"Thank you, Sergeant." The sergeant left the room.

Roth said, "Here we are, Dave. You read it. I already know the gist."

Boran read the message carefully, then said, "Sounds like quite a mess. What do you think?"

"The younger generation would very aptly refer to it as a fuck-up. Let's see what can be salvaged from the wreck," said Roth.

"Our first decision has to concern the mission. Do we tell them to go on with it, Max, or do we ask Moscow Cell to try and get our agents out pronto?"

Roth grimaced. "I think we should arrange to get them new IDs, and tell them to carry on. On one condition, of course—only if they're able to operate independently, and without too much involvement of the Cell."

"Yes, Max, I think you're right. Professor Nevsky sounds like a decent man. Yuri Slonin told us about him. As long as Nevsky can be convinced of the truth, Itzhak, Baruch, and Heidi should be able to pull the chestnuts out of the fire, and do a good job yet. After all, they did succeed in contacting the professor at once, and Heidi's friendship with his wife would seem to be a big asset."

"I agree," said Roth. "As soon as we can decently send a car for Slonin, I'll have him brought here and, with his help—his own expertise, signature evaluation, confirmation of photostats, etcetera—you can prepare the clearest and most convincing evidence for Nevsky you're capable of. I mean that, Dave. Really *convincing.*"

"Good." said Boran. "We should finish by this afternoon. Method of dispatch?"

Roth was slapping his hands together. "Diplomatic courier pouch to Bonn, by car to West Berlin. The usual agent will take it across to the East. If we add the plane journey to Moscow, the Cell ought to have the package by tomorrow lunchtime—at the latest."

Boran stared at his black pipe. "Now. To question two, Max. What about their IDs?"

"I think we'll have to design these to dovetail with their escape plans. East Germany, or any other Commie country, is out. That leaves us with Finland, if we're thinking of an overland route." Roth ran both of his hands across his bald head. "No. On second thought, foreign nationals don't travel to Finland in December, by road or rail via Russia—unless they have some very unusual and nontourist reasons for doing so."

Roth paced up and down on his short legs, thinking out loud. "I'd better have a word with our Ministry for Immigrant Absorption."

Boran lifted his pipe. "Why them? What have they got to do with SB policy?"

Roth explained. "After all, we're on speaking terms. And they do owe us a favor from our Vienna job a couple of months ago."

Roth was referring to a planned Arab Terrorist attack on the Vienna transit camp for immigrants en route to Israel from the Soviet Union. Prompt and eminently successful SB action had resulted in thwarting the enemy operation—and the capture of several Black September commandos already in Vienna.

"OK, Max. They do owe us a favor, but what can they do for us?"

Roth smiled mysteriously. "They can give us three immigrants."

Now Boran smiled. "I'm beginning to see your point. Yeah. We can bring them out with one of the transports. But the question is, do we fabricate three fictitious passports, exit permits, and so forth, or do we borrow the documents from three bonafide immigrants, and have a good cosmetics job done on our agents to fix their faces?"

Roth spoke slowly. "Well, we can't borrow all the documents they need at this end. There's the property export permit, for example, and, of course, the bottom part of the *rasresheniya* is taken off the immigrant, and filed there."

Roth was referring to the Russian permit issued to candidates for immigration to Israel a few weeks before departure, and at the time their passports are confiscated.

Also, Roth and Boran had to bear in mind that the KGB and Militia would check and recheck every document belonging to an immigrant bound for Israel. It would be all too easy for the Israelis to slip up somewhere along the line.

Max said as much.

"Yeah, Max. I agree that there could be nothing more watertight than borrowed sets of documents and permits issued in Moscow and not yet used. But that would mean asking three bonafide Russian Jews to forfeit their turns to immigrate. Perhaps, even worse—to face interrogation and punishment for losing their papers."

"True. But remember, Dave, Russia's a land notorious for its thieves. I've heard of scores of cases when passports and permits have been stolen from candidates for immigration."

Boran remained thoughtful for a few moments, smoking. Doubt and dissatisfaction were apparent in his steel-gray eyes.

Then he brightened, and said, "OK, why not—on condition we see to it that these bonafide documents are obtained by bonafide theft!"

Max Roth exploded with laughter. "If there's one thing our SB boys don't have to be taught, it's how to steal. You know that, Dave, as well as I do." He chuckled some more, "Your point would be well taken if it weren't for the problem of not wanting to have the authorities informed about three missing sets of documents. Especially so soon after they've commenced their hunt for three recently disappeared East Germans—probably enemy agents trying to get out of Russia. No, Dave, that wouldn't work."

Roth paused, and scratched his bald head. "We have to get what we need voluntarily from Jews prepared to make a very risky—and very brave—contribution, to the security of Israel. I don't believe we'll have to search far, or for long. The behavior of thousands of Russian Jews demonstrating at the Kremlin, at the Council of Soviets—fighting the Militia with their bare hands—has shown that they aren't short of heroism."

Boran's pipe had gone out. He struck a match and applied it to the bowl, drawing, but it wouldn't light. Finally he said, "I suppose you're right. Let the Cell handle it. We'll just have to stress the time factor in our message. First, the documents must be procured as soon as possible. Second, their theft must come to the notice of the Militia only after Heidi and our two boys are well out of the country. It'll be quite a job finding three candidates of the right age and size, but I'm sure the Cell will manage."

Over an early breakfast, Roth and Boran told Dr. Yuri Slonin about the new situation. The latter immediately set to work, together with Boran, preparing all the required evidence to satisfy Iliya Petrovitch Nevsky.

Simultaneously, Roth consulted the Ministry for Immigration Absorption who, with profound respect for Security Branch and its role in national defense, at once gave its consent and promise of cooperation.

Then Max Roth sent the first of several messages to the Moscow Cell, informing them about the decisions that had been taken.

This information included instructions for the Israeli Commando Unit, now lying low at No. 99 Kurumalinskaya Street; they were encouraged not to lose faith in the completion of their mission, and to be ready to carry on with their vital work as soon as they received the material for Nevsky and their new IDs.

After sending the message, Roth took out a violently-colored handkerchief, and blew his nose loudly.

The package for Professor Nevsky was in Heidi's hands at 11:30 on Sunday, December 10.

The Cell leader had explained to them about the strategy of procuring Russian documents and immigration permits.

This, they were told, would take another day or two. Their physical grooming, to fit the new IDs, would have to wait, too, since they should obviously try to look as similar as possible to the original ID owners.

News about the hue and cry which had followed in their fwake on the morning of December 9 was also relayed to them.

Militia and KGB men had stormed into the Hotel Berlin, ransacking the Israelis' rooms, and questioning every staff member and guest.

At the Convention Center and State University, files and registration lists had been carried off to KGB Headquarters.

Dr. Staniev had made a complete statement to the authorities the moment he had received a convincing negative reply to his inquiry from Heidelberg University.

Staniev had personally informed his friend Nevsky of the facts, and strongly impressed upon his interrogators that the professor had, no doubt, been the innocent victim of a charade whose sinister nature he couldn't possibly have suspected. But, to Heidi's consternation, Iliya and Vera were harrassed by KGB agents and, so far, Nevsky was so upset that he had been unable to attend the convention opening.

Vera was at home in the afternoon when her phone rang. Heidi introduced herself as: "your shopping friend."

"Oh, yes," Vera answered, recognizing Heidi's voice, but careful not to mention her name. "Iliya is distraught. So much has been going on. We don't know what to do. The police won't leave us alone."

She explained that two stern KGB officers had been to their home twice that day already, and asked questions for more than an hour each time.

They had not been at all kind or sympathetic.

The only reason the KGB hadn't taken them in and arrested them was because of the professor's reputation.

Vera and Iliya had given the KGB men a true account of the supper at the Explosion, and repeated everything that the Schuehlers and Herr Hansel had told them. The KGB men had refused to believe a word.

Vera and Iliya could add nothing more, except that

Vera had done some shopping with Ilse Schuehler, and that their conversation throughout the afternoon had been entirely devoted to fashions and the sights of Moscow.

Heidi said, "I'm so sorry about this, Vera. So sorry, believe me."

Vera Nevsky sighed, "I know. We both know how you feel."

"I'd like to see you," Heidi said.

"Lovely, dear," said Vera. "You know how delighted we always are to see *you*—and especially at a time like this."

They arranged to meet at the statue of Yuri the Long Arm on Gorki Street.

Cell Leader *99* was standing beside Heidi in the hallway. He had her suggest a place which would be easy to stake out and keep under observation.

Heidi felt sympathetic toward Vera, and terrible about what had happened. She wished she could do something helpful for the Nevskys, but there was nothing. She was certain nothing disastrous would be allowed to happen to them, because of the professor's position and his reputation, but still she felt bad.

Vera's arrival on Gorki Street, either unaccompanied or with the professor, would be carefully watched by the Israelis. And at the slightest suspicion that she was being followed, no contact would be made.

There was no intention to send Heidi to deliver the secret package. A female sympathizer would be asked to make contact with Vera. They could trust Nevsky to guard the package's contents carefully, and to destroy them the moment he deemed fit.

But Heidi and the others had already studied its shocking contents: stark, unequivocal evidence of a plot personally headed by Dr. George Habbash, leader of the Liberation Front, to commit mass murder in the towns and villages of Israel with the aid of Russia's most sophisticated materials for germ warfare.

There were highly technical scientific notations, handwritten, and signed by Professor Yuri Slonin, from which laymen could decipher just enough to understand that they were dealing with a new viscous suspension fluid, in which cholera, typhoid, and other bacilli, bacteria, and viruses, would survive for long periods of time in any climate—regardless of treatment by normal germicides.

There were photocopies of letters, minutes of meetings, and a handwritten memorandum, signed by Habbash and a Russian general.

Finally, Slonin had written a personal letter to Nevsky, recalling their many years of friendship, and appealing to him to do everything in his power to stop the Machiavellian plot.

"If this doesn't convince them," Baruch had said, "then nothing ever will."

Heidi looked at him and narrowed her eyes. "I know it will convince them."

"Which makes Nevsky our ally," Itzhak added.

"I hope so. For all our sakes," Cell Leader *99* said. "Because there's certainly no other way that I can see of getting to those containers."

"If they're concentrated in the cellar on Mokhavaya Street," Heidi said, "Professor Nevsky will deal with them himself."

Itzhak said, "If not, he'll just have to let us know the time and place of transportation, and we—or anyway, our boys—will do the job. We'll have to."

"Amen to that," said *99*.

Around four o'clock on the afternoon of Sunday, December 10, a nondescript young woman approached Vera Nevsky at the foot of the statue of Yuri the Long Arm and asked her to come for a walk with her.

Vera, having innocently expected Ilse in person, though perhaps disguised, was startled.

But the stranger succeeded in allaying Vera's doubts when she handed her a note from Heidi which mentioned the menu of the supper they had been served at the Explosion.

Then, when they had walked down as far as Nikita Gates, a man came up to them, spoke a few quiet words with the stranger, and then handed the package containing the documents over to Vera Nevsky.

As if it were a bomb, and might go off at any moment . . .

If a KGB agent had been nearby, he would have become immediately suspicious.

. . . 15

When Professor Iliya Nevsky received this material that night, he locked himself in his study and asked Vera to make sure he would not be disturbed.

Almost an hour later, he came out—pale, and obviously profoundly shaken.

"What is it, darling?" Vera asked him, shocked by his appearance.

"I hardly dare tell you!"

"But you must, Iliya," said Vera.

"Yes," he said. "I must."

"Were they right? Are we really helping the Arabs pollute their water?" Vera asked.

The professor stared at her for a long moment without blinking.

"Yes, Vera. There's no doubt about it. Yuri Slonin would never lie to me." He shook his head. "Besides, the evidence speaks for itself. I'm shocked. How could they do this to me? I haven't deserved this dishonor."

He shook his head, blinking rapidly now, then stared at her intently. "I'm a Russian, through and through. I believe in my country. You know that. But I also consider myself a humanitarian. I am a moral man. You know I am!"

They sat down together, holding hands.

The professor was, above all, a man of principle and conscience. He loved his country; that was true. But even more, he loved humanity. He had dedicated himself to serve mankind in the sacred name of science.

A plot to misuse his services for solely destructive purposes—completely alien to his philosophy, and divorced from many overriding considerations of national security—was a profound shock, a traumatic source of disillusionment.

Vera was hesitant. "What will you do, Iliya?"

The Professor shook his head and clenched his hands. "The only thing I can do—nullify the effects of my work on Mokhavaya Street; destroy the materials and, if need be, also the formula, my notations, and the instruments, chemicals—everything!" He spread his hands, then brought them together forcefully.

"But they'll send you away. You know they will! It may mean the end of your career and your work . . . all your hopes and plans!"

Professor Nevsky turned toward his wife and looked at her. He tried to force a smile. "Please try to understand me, Vera. Bear with me, and forgive me, please. I would rather end my days in the uranium mines of the Urals than allow myself to be used in such a shameful manner. Someone has made a farce of my work. I can't allow it, and I won't. You know me well enough to know that. You know me too well to believe that anything—or anyone—can persuade me to proceed any other way."

Vera understood her husband exactly.

The professor shook his head. "Now I'm beginning to regret my research. But I, and my assistant, did our work only after receiving the assurances of the highest authorities that we were merely part of an overall plan to maintain that vital balance of power between us and our enemies—which is, unhappily, the only guarantee for world peace."

He stood up. His shoulders were hunched.

"All right, Iliya!" Vera said. "The Israelis have come to Moscow specifically to prevent this pollution plot from succeeding. It's their job. You must understand that. They're experts on destruction. You are not. Help them, yes. Open doors. Anything! Only, please, don't perform the destruction yourself!"

Her beautiful face was frowning. Her eyes were pleading with him.

Finally, Nevsky said: "Yes." And he continued in a new, less emotional, and coldly determined tone of voice. "There might be a way of saving the laboratories and valuable equipment, and yet getting rid of the materials destined to be sent to the Middle East." Then, with even more assurance, he slowly smiled at his wife. "And, it would also be the one possible way of saving myself. Of saving us."

Tears filled Vera's eyes. They were tears of relief. She stood, not taking her eyes off her husband, and embraced him.

The three Israeli agents sat in the small kitchen of the Cell's apartment on Kurumalinskaya Street.

It was Monday, December 11, their third day in hiding. Time was dragging heavily, and lack of physical exercise was making them alternately drowsy and irritable.

For Heidi and Itzhak, it was especially trying.

Their confinement, instead of lessening their sexual desire, had heightened it. It was cold and uncomfortable in their room, but they did the best they could for relief. Love had its way.

They were forever touching, holding, grasping, brushing against each other, each trying to let the other know how he felt. And in the darkness of their room at night, they explained their love in whispers. But even that was not enough.

Their sexual embraces were sometimes savage, brutal, each trying to give the other reinforcement and strength.

Itzhak had never felt such desire. It was all-engulfing. If he touched Heidi at all, he immediately had an erection. He wanted to rape her. He wanted to love her tenderly.

The three Israelis had neither seen nor heard from the outside world during the past twenty-four hours, since the package had been taken for delivery to Vera Nevsky.

Cell Leader 99 had not come to see them since the arrival of the message from Boran and Roth. He had told them he would be kept busy arranging their new documents and, when he finally appeared again, their first thought was that he was already bringing them with him.

In fact, however, *99* brought news from Professor Nevsky. The cell had telephoned his house the night before, and received his carefully worded consent to co-operate.

No names were mentioned. They spoke of the containers of cholera germs by alluding to them as "canned soup."

The Cell leader had met Nevsky outside Frunzenskaya Underground station an hour early and, over a glass of tea at the buffet, worked out a schedule of further meetings.

"We didn't have very much time to talk," *99* told the three Israelis. "But if I got his meaning correctly, Nevsky is trying to find out the dates and methods of transportation. Of course, he's in no position to ask outright questions. He isn't supposed to know anything about the destination of the containers. What he probably expects is that just before the materials from Mokhavaya Street are removed, he's going to be asked to check them for leakage, or perhaps test samples for possible deterioration. Damn it all! I didn't know what to do. I asked him how long the 'soup' has been in storage already, and he said about three months. They've got enough for the entire operation. They're not making any more. The professor is now working on other 'canned goods,' as we called them."

"I wonder why they haven't delivered the stuff to Habbash yet," said Heidi.

"It may be a question of political pressure. The Kremlin likes to keep it's Communist allies in line. They don't want to repeat mistakes of the past when they gave their allies all they asked for, only to get kicked on their asses, with no gratitude for their help."

Itzhak spoke up, "They'll have to deliver damn soon," he said. "If Habbash, Black September, or Al Fatah are to be kept out of the Peking camp."

Baruch said, "It's a bloody mess. But in my opinion, it's mainly a question of manpower. The Arabs have been running short of 'soldiers,' as they call them—active combatants, and as long as they can show next to no serious terrorist activity, they're not getting their minimum quota of fresh volunteers."

It was discussions such as this which kept time from standing still. On the afternoon of Thursday, December 14, *99* returned—after a three-day absence—carrying a briefcase stuffed with papers and documents.

99 took out the documents in three separate sets, each held together by a thick elastic band.

He handed the first one to Itzhak. It was marked: Samuel Meiersohn.

The second informed Heidi that she was now Paula Ginsberg. The last went to Baruch, now Misha Lipsky.

The outstanding document was the *rasresheniya,* the exit permit, issued only the day before.

On it, besides the description of full personal information, were two copies of a passport photo—attached to the upper and lower section, a perforation enabling the K.P.P. Border Patrol at the airport to detach the two parts and retain the lower for "Internal Filing" with KGB. There were also permits to take out of the country and a personal allowance of 120 United States dollars, to be purchased at the bank for 90 rubles.

Heidi looked up with a smile. "Paula Ginsberg is better than Ilse Schuehler," she said.

"Lipsky isn't such an improvement on Hansel, I admit, but Misha at least sounds less German than Fritz," Baruch said with a grin.

Itzhak, who was studying his new ID with intense interest, remarked sadly, "I don't feel like joking. I'm wondering about the three flesh-and-blood people whose papers they really are. This must be tough on them."

"Believe me, it is," *99* said. "But they want you to know they're doing this wholeheartedly." His voice softened. "They wish you luck, too. Their immigration date is set up for thirty days from the date of issuance, so naturally they still have a glimmer of hope that you'll get out in time for them to report the thefts, and appeal for new documents to get on the transport to Vienna." He sighed, and smiled one of his rare smiles. His eyes were misty.

"It should also interest you to know that the three donors are old friends. They'll claim to have been pick-pocketed in the Underground on the same trip, traveling together. To make it as easy on them as possible, we'll try to arrange a rash of thefts on the Underground the same day. That way it'll look like an organized operation by the illegal immigration syndicate which is known to exist in Moscow."

Baruch said, "But—assuming we get through okay—won't there be duplication?"

99 scowled. You mean—won't your exits also be registered under their names?" He paused. "Yes, they will. But we're counting on the KGB to figure out very quickly that the descriptions in their rogues' gallery of Heinrich and Ilse Schuehler and Fritz Hansel also fit the physical features of Meiersohn, Ginsberg, and Lipsky. They're famous for putting two and two together very soon. And the other documents and robberies should make it appear to be just a well organized operation by a foreign intelligence network to get you out of the country." *99* paused again, and scratched his chin. "And by that time, you'll be safe."

"We hope," Itzhak said. "Anyhow, please thank the three donors for us."

"I will," *99* said.

Heidi had continued to study her papers. "Back to being single again. Miss Paula Ginsberg. She's as least as beautiful as me, and a year younger to boot. What's wrong with her love life?"

Itzhak grinned, "There's probably too much of it, not too little. That's one way of staying unmarried in Russia."

"We'll fix her up when she comes to Israel," Heidi said, turning to Baruch. "What about it?"

99 spoke up. "This is hardly the time and place for matchmaking."

They spent the remainder of the day learning and

memorizing the data and biographical details of their new IDs. By evening, they were addressing one another by their new names.

Heidi and Itzhak had spent much time working on their colloquial Russian. A Cell member had brought them a Russian grammar and a record player. Now they threw themselves into the effort with a will.

All day long, language-instruction records played straight into their ears, through large rubber-padded earphones. *"Progaliste, spassivo, kharasho,"* and many other useful everyday words became familiar, and when the Jewish-Russian hairdresser and cosmetician set to work on them on Friday—from morning until late evening—they were delighted to find that their vocabulary already sufficed to ask and answer many simple questions.

Their hair and eye colors had to be changed. The shape of Itzhak's mustache and the style of Heidi's hair were also changed.

After their metamorphosis into Meiersohn, Ginsberg, and Lipsky, a new set of passport photos was made. These would be substituted for the donors' by the Cell's expert forger. The new photos on the *rasresheniya* might later on be cross-checked with the "donors'" passports, already on the KGB file, *99* told them. But that would happen only after the report of the thefts and help to convince the authorities of their innocence.

By Saturday evening, *99*—who, like a captain aboard his ship, considered himself temporarily in charge of his guests—felt it would be safe to launch Ginsberg, Meiersohn, and Lipsky into the open stream of Kurumaliskaya Street.

Should an unavoidable conversation develop between them and other passersby, Baruch, alias Misha Lipsky, would be there to do the talking. Militia were, of course, to be scrupulously avoided if possible.

The three Israelis gratefully stretched their legs and filled their lungs with the fresh, cold air.

The weather had improved, and the dry four-degrees-below-zero temperature no longer seemed so inhospitable. In fact, a brisk walk three times around the block had an invigorating effect on them all.

But they talked very little, wholly intent on exercising their cramped and sluggish muscles.

. . . 16

Their exercise periods were repeated and extended on Sunday and Monday. Several times they were passed by Militia, usually patroling in pairs, wearing their smart dark uniforms with red borders and blue epaulettes, and usually bearing the noncommissioned officers' insignia of white strips.

Sometimes the epaulettes were of silver, and worn by officers, but the Israelis were not stopped once, and they felt certain that they were not followed by plainclothesmen.

"This is more like it," Heidi said. "It's great to be reborn."

Itzhak was in agreement.

They visited Lenin Library and the Old Riding Parade.

They rode on the splendid Moscow Underground. Heidi and Itzhak tried out phrases like "*Jdiyeh nachodizia?*" ("Where is this?") And the longer variation: "*Sprasho gdiyeh nachodizia Uliza?*" ("Where is that street, please?"), pointing at a paper with an address written on it.

They strolled along Moskva River, and crossed some of its innumerable bridges.

For a brief time, they almost felt like tourists.

On Tuesday, December 19, they were shaken out of their complacency by *99*, who brought them a message from Nevsky. The professor had just been asked by the relevant authorities to give a final check to the fatal containers for removal on the 24th.

"That's it!" Itzhak exclaimed. "Does he know where they're to be taken?"

99 shook his head slowly, and replied. "Yes . . . at least to some extent. A van will take them to Sheremetyevo Airport. Nevsky will accompany the containers, and see that they're carefully loaded on the plane. And don't ask me where the plane is flying to. Not even the professor knows that. Still, since it's sure to be in the Middle East, our plotting station should be able to pick it up and keep it on the beam—as long as you can inform them in advance about the time of departure, type of aircraft, and anything else you can find out."

Baruch said, "We did hear you say 'you', didn't we?"

"Yeah, that's right. Holiday time is over. You've all changed beautifully, and now it's back to work."

"You sound just like Roth and Boran," Itzhak remarked.

"When are you throwing us out, and where?" Baruch wanted to know.

99 grinned. "Who said we were throwing you out? This place has served you comfortably these past ten days, so you can stay and work from here. Don't worry, this isn't the Cell headquarters. We wouldn't have risked bringing you there. It's just one of several places we hole up in."

"Thank you for letting us stay," Heidi said. "Do we rate pillows and mattresses by now—not to mention bedsheets."

"You rate them, Heidi, but you won't get them," *99* said. "This flat is supposed to serve as a meeting place for a poetry appreciation club."

Itzhak smiled. "So that's why you weren't afraid to carry records, books, and briefcases filled with papers in and out!"

"Right you are," *99* said.

"When can we meet Nevsky?" Heidi asked him.

"Tomorrow. Here are your exact instructions."

99 handed a sheet of paper to Itzhak. "Nevsky will be at the Kiev railway station restaurant. We're putting a tail on him to see if he's being followed. I'll tell you now, apropos, there's never been any sign that he's under surveillance. If the area is clean, our man will give you the sign. Walk straight in, find a table, and sit down. Don't give any sign to Nevsky. It'll be interesting to see if he recognizes you at once. If he doesn't come over to join you after five minutes, it means he hasn't identified you, and you can signal him. All the details are here. Please memorize and destroy them."

They took a bus for part of the way, but approached the station on foot.

One of the Cell members was waiting for them outside the station, and walked on a few meters ahead of them to the restaurant entrance.

Unobtrusively, he gave them the go-ahead sign. They entered, at once recognizing Professor Nevsky at a table by the rear wall, far from the glass windows looking out onto the station platform.

He was pale.

They found an empty table about halfway between the entrance and Nevsky, and sat down. Their guide had disappeared for the moment, but later they noticed him again, hovering nearby.

Most of the tables were occupied. A fairly large crowd clustered at the bar.

None of the Israelis spoke.

Five long minutes went by in silence. The professor did not rise to approach them.

Heidi, following instructions, signaled Nevsky on her way back from the restroom. He rose and followed her. It all looked natural. An old, or new, female acquaintance accompanied by two other men, had spotted a third friend and invited him to join them at their table.

"These are my good friends, Samuel Meiersohn, and Misha Lipsky—Professor Iliya Petrovitch Nevsky," Heidi said. She conducted the introductions in faultless Russian.

From that point on, all the talking for the Israelis was done by Baruch, with Itzhak and Heidi putting an occasional comment into Russian just for the sake of appearances.

Baruch spoke up, "I guess we can talk safely here, if we keep our voices down."

"Yes, Comrade Lipsky."
"Great. Is the twenty-fourth still the day?"
"That's right."
"Are all the canned goods being exported?"
"Yes."
"Our usual countries?"
"Yes. One specifically."

Baruch had been dawdling with his pen on a paper napkin. Now he wrote on it: Syria, Lebanon, Iraq.

Nevsky took his own pen from his pocket and casually crossed Syria and Lebanon off the list.

"Are we making any more soup, perhaps?" Baruch asked.

"No. None at all. And not likely to be in the near future."

"What time will you have to be at 'M'?"

Baruch had to ask this question twice. Then the professor understood that "M" stood for Mokhavaya Street.

"Oh . . . yes. About two-thirty in the afternoon."

"Who's driving the van?"

"Is that important?"

"Very important."

"I'll have to let you know."

"Will your friends all be wearing uniforms?"

"No, comrade. This is a civilian job. Perhaps the driver. He might. In a day or two, you'll know."

"Who's going with the van?"

"Only myself and the driver. It's a small number of cans, weighing no more than twenty-five kilos, with the crate."

"Does the crate have handles?"

"Usually, two people carry it. Yes, it has handles."

"Since the consignment is going by air freight, will it take a long time going through customs and other red tape at the airport, do you think?"

"No. Not at all, comrade. It should get there by four o'clock, and the plane is due to take off at four-forty."

"That's convenient."

While they sipped their tea, they talked also about the welcome winter sunshine, and the superior performance of the new Jiguli cars that were just coming off the production lines.

When they parted, Heidi quietly sent her warmest regards to Vera—certainly the most straightforward and sincere words spoken since this meeting had begun.

At their apartment, *99* and the other two Cell members, were waiting for a full report, and the Israelis gave it at once.

99 seemed elated, in his own calm fashion. "Excellent!" he said. "The plan is taking shape nicely. We'll be able to supply you with explosives or whatever you might need. Of course, we can't take any direct part in the operation. That's clear, I hope."

"Quite clear," Itzhak said. "But what happens right after we blast or hijack these cans. Do we come straight back here?"

"Sure, if you can manage it. Why not? We won't be around to advise you. So it's up to you."

Baruch seemed reflective. "Then we'll have to play this pretty much by ear," he said. "A lot'll depend on the speed with which the alarm is sounded, and how far it goes. To hole up here is pointless, if we've been tailed."

"You're now discussing stage five of the operation," said Heidi. "Why don't we start with the first bridge we'll have to cross. How do we get next to those soup cans?"

"Very pragmatic of you, dear Paula," Itzhak said. "But for that, we must wait until we hear again from Nevsky, particularly about that truck driver. Basically, there are three points at which we can intercept the cargo. One, at its starting out point on Mokhavaya Street. Two, anywhere along the route to Sheremetyevo. And three, at the airport."

He paused. "At point one, the main problems are the additional men on the spot. When Nevsky stresses that this is a civilian job, I translate this into a KGB job. The professor would not have used a term like '*job*' for the operation otherwise, would he, Misha?"

"No, he likely wouldn't. He'd use the derogatory

Russian word for *'job'* as opposed to *'work.'* I agree Samuel. He meant KGB."

99 spoke up. "That makes sense," he said. "On an operation like this, every effort will be made not to attract the attention of the public eye. The authorities have good reason to be convinced that only they and the top chiefs in the Arab command are fully in the know. Even scientists like Nevsky were only allowed to possess those parts of the secret, which could not be kept from them. The business of transporting the containers to the plane will be played down—not over-dramatized. No Militia or Army in uniforms. The professor will probably be told that the material is simply being shipped for permanent safe storage in Outer Mongolia, or somewhere."

Baruch looked up. "Yeah," he said. "I agree. And to all this we can add the safe assumption that the KGB hasn't the slightest reason for connecting the disappearance of three mysterious East German delegates to the Moscow Scientific Research Convention to the impending transportation of germ warfare containers to the Middle East. So there simply wouldn't be any logic in tight security."

"And least of all," Itzhak said, "security along the route from central Moscow to fairly distant Sheremetyevo."

99 said, "That seems to point the way for your operational strategy."

"Yes, it does," Baruch said. "But let's be patient for another day or two, until Professor Nevsky sends us his next message."

"Don't worry, comrades," *99* said with a smile. "He won't even have to send it. We'll be right there on his doorstep, ready to take it away from him."

. . . 17

The professor's message arrived well within the time limit he had set for himself—late on the evening of Thursday, December 21.

It contained only two points. One: no changes regarding previous reported timetable. Two: driver to be a former KGB operator, now of pensionable age, retained on odd-job basis. No uniform.

Itzhak turned to *99* and said, "OK, comrade. You promised us the necessary equipment for the twenty-fourth. Here's what we need: two cars, with Moscow registration plates. A Volga and a Jiguli. Make sure the Volga can carry a fairly large crate with no bother. And please make sure that the trunk is empty. Tool box, jack, spare tires, and so forth can go on the back-seat floor. The Jiguli can be a regular sports model built for speed. Get us the most common color seen in Moscow."

"Will do," said *99*. "Maroon and beige. Black is getting much rarer nowadays. What else do you want?"

"Well," Itzhak said, "an explosive charge. Gelignite would do fine. Plastics, but simple TNT is also OK. A delayed time device, with a spare battery, adjustable to an hour. Two gas pistols. I'd also like a Browning nine millimeter automatic, if you can manage it."

"Can do," *99* said. "What else?"

"The ordinary antiburglar variety gas pistol will be fine. Three sets of handcuffs, a couple of kilos of two-inch nails, three hand grenades. That's about all. Yes."

"No problem. You'll have everything up here the day after tomorrow except the cars, of course. Those you'll get—parked handy—by two p.m. on the twenty-fourth. I'll let you know exactly where later."

When *99* had said he would have everything ready on the 23rd, he had immediately began to make calculations in weight, volume, and distribution. And that particular Saturday would, therefore, go down in Heidi's personal diary, reconstructed from incoherent and disconnected notes much later, as "The Day of Tantalus"—her learned and special reference to the ever-thirsty, ever-hungry god.

In the morning, Cell No. 1 brought a large bag of "freshly baked rolls"—four rolls at the top, and two kilos of nails beneath.

Then *99* arrived with "fresh fruit"—three large juicy apples from the deep-freeze counter of GUM covering three hand grenades of similar size, as well as the Browning 9mm pistol and a shoulder holster. Cell No. 2 brought a beautiful homemade cake, consisting of a thin layer of dough on top, several cups of buttercream spread on all sides, and a two-pound explosive charge in the center. A box of chocolates presented to her by *99* in the evening, "to celebrate the eve of your successful operation," contained the two gas pistols, the handcuffs, and the timing device for the bomb.

"With all this going on," Heidi later wrote, "There was, of course, no thought for bringing us anything to appease our appetites. So we dined on four rolls, three apples, and buttercream."

Sunday, December 24, dawned cloudless, cold, and dry.

In places where the snow had not already been swept away by the wind, by the brooms of house-keepers, or by the mechanical means of the Moscow municipality, it was frozen crystal-hard, and smooth.

Baruch, as usual, had slept soundly, as if he hadn't a worry in the world.

But Itzhak and Heidi, in the neighboring room, had spent a restless and not too productive night.

Now that the climax of their dangerous mission was

only hours away, both came face to face with the grim realization that this might well be their last night together for a long time to come, if not forever.

Before their marriage, each had lived his own life. Each had taken their occupational hazards in stride. They had led solitary existences, teamwork and adventure being substituted for marriage.

The death or injury of a friend was sad, but bearable—both as possibilities and in retrospect. Even one's own death could be contemplated with a daredevil's contemptuous eye.

But now they were facing the risk of double-indemnity. They each were suddenly possessed of two lives to gamble with, and lose.

"Remember your promise—no unnecessary risks. And do what I tell you," Itzhak told Heidi for the third time.

They had been given two specially drawn maps of Moscow and the Scheremetyvo area. On it were marked the Old University Building on Mokhavaya Street (now officially named Marx Prospekt), Lenin Library, Srvedlov, Manyezh, and Red Square; major thoroughfares such as Gorki Street, Lenin Prospekt, Sadovoyeh Koltzo, Gorkova Prospekt, Sovietsky Boulevard, Chkalovskaya Street as well as those secondary roads forming the easiest exit to the northwest, with a drawn-in red line marking the most likely route that the van would follow from Mokhavaya Street to the airport. It was a possible hour's slow drive, considering the delicate nature of the cargo in the van. A blue line marked the recommended route.

The separate Sheremetyevo map had markings specially drawn for the operation—in particular, Militia checkpoints, entrances and exits, parking and loading areas for the regular passenger or transport flights, luggage inspection, and K.P.P. border control points.

Of course, no one could even guess where or how a special plane to carry such a cargo might be parked, prior to unscheduled takeoff.

The three Security Branch agents had spent the early evening memorizing this map.

At five minutes before 2:00 p.m. on December 24, Itzhak left the house, looked left and right, and walked toward the parked Volga. At thirty-second intervals, Heidi and Baruch followed. Baruch joined Itzhak in the Volga, and Heidi settled herself comfortably behind the wheel of the Jiguli. This had been an almost last-minute decision.

Their first plan was to let Heidi go with Itzhak, and give the task of cover, or decoy car, to the more experienced Baruch.

However, they had finally agreed on the other division of forces for two overriding considerations. To have the husband and his wife in the same car might prove a psychological handicap; in the event of violence, they would be more likely to cover for each other and thus reduce their combined firepower. Secondly, the Volga was the car designed to receive the cargo—if it could not be destroyed inside the van (and that might not be feasible, out of consideration for Nevsky, who would be sitting with the driver).

Without saying so, Itzhak had thought about a third contingency—the probability of the Volga becoming the primary target of a Russian counterattack, if it developed.

"We're taking one hell of a chance," Baruch had said.

No one gave him an argument.

Cruising slowly, in accordance with their planned approach routes, the two cars arrived at parallel sides of Mokhavaya Street and pulled up at 2:25 p.m.

Heidi remained in her Jiguli, and the two men—armed only with their pistols carried in shoulder holsters—began to reconnoiter in the vicinity of the Old University Building.

"You think we'll make it?" Baruch asked.

"Look!" said Itzhak.

A small closed van—the type that might normally be used to deliver newspapers or bread—was pulled up to a side entrance.

Its driver was standing near the hood of the engine, probably on lookout. Two other men in civilian clothes watched with apparent nonchalance from across the street. At exactly 2:30 p.m., two powerfully-built porters wearing blue overalls carried a wooden crate, measuring about three feet in length and breadth, and two feet in height, from the entrance.

They were accompanied by two white-coated men, one of whom Baruch and Itzhak immediately recognized as Professor Nevsky.

"Here we go!" Itzhak whispered.

By 2:40 p.m., the crate was loaded and secured in the back of the van.

Professor Nevsky shook hands with his colleague and entered the cab, together with the driver. The two porters went back into the building without waiting, but the remaining white-clad figure stood on the sidewalk, and waved good-bye until the van turned the corner.

The Israelis noticed that the two civilians across the street got into a black Volga, which looked more solid than the one they themselves were driving.

"Custom-made, I'd think," Itzhak remarked.

"Yeah—it's heavier in frame and bodywork," Baruch said.

"That should slow it down."

"Only if the engine hasn't been specially made to fit the body."

Then the Israelis pulled away from the curb, drove around the single block, and passed Heidi's still stationary car. They turned right along a narrow but traffic-free road running parallel to Mokhavaya. A second turning to the right took them through a lane that was obviously not meant for car traffic, but which had been clearly marked by the blue line on the map.

"This looks tricky," said Baruch.

"It is tricky."

The shortcut brought them back to the street which would be the most likely route northwest to the suburb that had to be passed through before reaching the highway leading out to the airport. They drove another mile and stopped at an unobtrusive spot on the asphalt apron.

Baruch was at the wheel. He said, "If we've calculated the distance in speed correctly, the van should be coming up behind, just about . . ." He glanced at the watch on the dashboard, waited about a minute and a half, and then, without looking around, said, *"now!"*

Five seconds later, the van, driven at a leisurely pace, drove by them.

"Not too bad. Maybe better next time," Itzhak said with a grin.

Ten yards behind the van was the black custom Volga. They caught a quick glimpse of the two men inside. Both had been wearing raincoats that seemed too thin for this climate and European-style Trilby hats pulled down over their eyes.

Fifty yards behind came Heidi, who turned her head in recognition.

They did not "join the line," as Baruch jokingly put it, but drove along a side street, which took them away from the road traveled by the others.

Turning to the left brought them parallel, and they now risked a spurt of real speed. Then to the left once more for an intersection with the main road. Their luck seemed to hold, and they had a green traffic light for their right turn.

Itzhak, looking behind, could see the van stopped by the red light—only the second vehicle from the intersection.

"That was a close one!" he remarked. "If we'd hit the red instead of them, it might have thrown our war plan badly out of gear."

From then on, they kept ahead. For twenty minutes more, they drove between blocks of tenements and offices, but gradually these massive structures became fewer and fewer. Soon they were passing through stretches of open countryside, with old brick farmhouses indicating that this had been a green-belt area up until quite a short while ago.

Baruch also remarked on the surprisingly large number of single-story houses entirely constructed of wood—a sight not expected so near a metropolis the size of Moscow.

By 3:20 p.m., they had reached a long straight stretch of road going up a mild incline. This gradient was, however, steep enough so that when it turned into a dip on the other side, their car was able to pull up alongside and park.

Vehicles coming up the rise would not be able to see it before reaching the top, only twenty yards away.

Itzhak said to Baruch, "You'd better get out and have a look around."

"OK."

Baruch got out and placed himself at a lookout position from which he could signal Itzhak.

The black Volga made the mission more complicated. Thinking back, Itzhak was surprised at himself and the others for banking so heavily on a completely unprotected transfer of the secret containers to the airport. Their "tail" car was, of course, putting Heidi into a more difficult position, too, since she would have to let the strangers' Volga remain between her and the van.

Three minutes went by before Baruch spotted the van coming toward them—still over half a mile away.

Fortunately, there was no other vehicle between them and their target.

At Baruch's signal, Itzhak drove the car back onto the highway. Baruch remained standing at the roadside, showing two fingers above his head. Itzhak responded by driving to the second of five lanes. Driving slowly, he tilted the sack containing the nails out of the window. It was empty after twenty yards, and he pulled over to the apron.

This maneuver had taken fifteen seconds—ten seconds less than it took the van to reach the top of the rise.

Baruch had stepped out of sight behind a tree.

The vehicle was traveling too fast to brake before its wheels went over the two kilograms of nails. Two of its tires punctured and deflated within five seconds.

In planning this move, the Israelis had hoped the driver would not see the nails, and would remain unaware of the reason for the punctures until he got off to inspect his tires.

However, the man behind the wheel turned out to be more alert than the ordinary driver. As a result, he did the one thing that probably saved the day for his attackers. Once he saw the massive nails, he jammed down his foot on the brakes, a reaction that couldn't prevent his van from skidding across the nails, but which caused the black Volga—just coming over the top of the incline only fifteen yards behind—to smash with a tear of metal into the rear of the van at a speed of thirty-five miles an hour.

"Terrific!" Heidi shouted.

Her safety distance of fifty yards, plus her knowledge of what lay ahead, enabled her to slow, swerve to the right, and pull up almost alongside the two damaged vehicles.

She would have perferred to jump out and join the fray, but she recalled her promise. And, for the moment, she saw no reason to break it.

But she was very worried.

Itzhak and Baruch had decided to act in unison, and simultaneously, against the van driver and his escorts in the Volga.

The Israelis had not counted on the professor to play any part in the attack, but they had underestimated his outraged honor and pride.

The driver saw the two Israelis coming toward him. When Nevsky saw the driver pull a heavy automatic pistol from his pocket, he decided to act.

He had no experience whatsoever, but would not let the Israelis be shot down.

Fortunately, the driver's window was shut tight against the cold and he had to turn his back to the professor in order to roll it down and bring his weapon to bear. This gave Iliya Petrovitch Nevsky his opportunity.

He was shaking. In his righthand pocket, he carried a heavy bunch of keys, including some of the old massive variety used for his private office and laboratory.

Without hesitation, he drew them out, balled them in

his fist, leaned forward, and struck a blow with all his might to the wrist of the driver's gun hand.

The pistol flew from the man's grasp, and he gave out with a string of howling curses.

Itzhak had already been at the door of the van, but it was locked from inside. Professor Nevsky's action had given Itzhak time to smash the window with his pistol butt, and to point the gun at the driver's temple.

Meanwhile, Baruch had no difficulty in overpowering the one conscious passenger of the black Volga. Its hood was smashed and its windscreen shattered into tiny fragments. The head of the other rider had gone clear through the glass. He was both unconscious and covered with blood. The driver had received a sharp blow on his chest from the steering wheel, and was groaning and clutching himself, but Baruch did not think he was seriously injured. Within seconds, Baruch had the driver handcuffed and in the Israelis' Volga.

Itzhak had forced his prisoner to step down from the van.

"Professor Nevsky," he said, "run as far away as you can. Right now! Run!"

Nevsky complied without a word.

A few cars had passed by on the opposite side of the highway without stopping to investigate what, at a glance, appeared no more than the sort of road accident one sees almost daily.

One car did stop for a moment, and its driver asked: "Anyone hurt?"

To which Baruch made a nonchalant negative reply.

As soon as the car had driven on, Baruch tried to pry open the back of the van, but its doors were tightly jammed by the Volga.

Itzhak climbed back into the cab after telling Heidi to guard the handcuffed man inside their own Volga. Itzhak was carrying the explosive charge and timing device.

"Hey, Baruch!" he shouted. "This is a break." He was referring to a window connecting the back of the cab with the cargo compartment.

After sliding back the two metal plates, there was an

opening large enough to insert the bomb and place it right on top of the crate with the containers.

Itzhak had only a moment to decide on the length of time he should allow before the bomb would explode. Already another vehicle, this one a heavy truck, had pulled up beside them, and its driver had noticed the bleeding, unconscious man behind the broken windscreen. Hoping his decision was wise, Itzhak set the timing device for five minutes, and jumped back onto the road on the side away from the truck.

This activity inside the van had remained unnoticed. When Itzhak signaled to Baruch, they both ran back to their car.

Baruch's voice was low. "Now all we need is luck!"

. . . 18

The truck driver was shouting after them.

"Hey! Hey, you! You can't leave an injured man!"

Baruch turned and shouted. "Take him to a hospital yourself. This isn't our accident."

Itzhak was already in front with Heidi, and Baruch was getting in back with their two prisoners.

"That truck driver's got four minutes to go," Itzhak told Baruch significantly. "Say something to hurry him up!"

"Can't we take the unconscious man in here, too?" asked Heidi.

"We probably could, but that means dealing with three prisoners, and one of them God know's how badly hurt."

To their relief, the truck driver had got out and was removing the unconscious man from the Volga.

"You mother-fucking bastards!" he screamed at them. "I've got your number, and I'll get the Militia after you! I promise you that!"

It was now that Itzhak acted. He knew he had to do something. He leaped from the car, his Browning automatic in his right hand.

The truck driver saw it, ran across the road, and leaped the fence.

"Who the hell *are* you?" the truck driver shouted.

"Who are *you*?" Itzhak shouted, advancing.

But he already knew. The truck driver was kneeling, holding a gun.

"KGB," he said.

Itzhak had felt all along that they couldn't get away so easily.

He fired the Browning twice, but missed the man both times.

But the truck driver turned and began running over toward a hillock of snow, plowing through the heavy powder.

Itzhak went after the man fast. He should have realized earlier that the truck driver might be with the KGB, but one thing he knew now for sure: the truck driver was frightened—frightened of being killed.

And one other thing Itzhak knew: he must kill the truck driver.

He came over the top of the knoll in a bound, and met with a fusillade of bullets. The slugs seemed to tear the air and rip at the ground all around him, but none struck home.

Itzhak fell flat on the ground, thrusting the Browning out before him. The truck driver was immediately in his sights.

"Don't!' he whimpered.

Itzhak fired five times, raising his right wrist with his left hand in a tight grip.

The slugs struck the KGB man—the truck driver—directly in the chest.

For a moment he just stood there, as if admiring the snow, the landscape, the sky. Then dark blood gushed from his chest, and he sprawled in a heap. Itzhak didn't wait. He turned and ran back across the field and up to the car.

"Let's go!" he exclaimed, even before he closed his door.

He slammed his foot on the accelerator and they sped away.

The Jiguli was left behind, in accordance with their plan. It had been brought along as an emergency measure, had not been required, and contained nothing that could lead the authorities to the Kurumalinskaya Street Cell.

Inside their Volga, there were weapons and other items of equipment which would either have to be jettisoned or returned to the Cell—whichever would prove less dangerous for those involved.

"What about Nevsky?" asked Heidi.

"He's clever, and if he doesn't panic—and I don't think he will—he isn't in any danger. I warned him about the explosion," Itzhak said. "Later, someone will pick him up and, if he plays it right, he'll be looked upon as a lucky victim of our attack who managed to get away."

"And how about this gentleman here?" Baruch asked, pointing at the van driver whose wrist the professor had struck.

"Well—for the moment, he's where he can't do Nevsky any harm. Let's take one problem at a time, shall we? First, we get rid of this car before someone reports us to the Militia for not giving aid to an unfortunate traffic accident victim. Also, it can't be much longer before those nails on the road are discovered, plus the explosion inside the van. Not to mention the unconscious man in the Volga." He paused. "And there's a body over there, beyond that knoll, that they'll find soon."

"You killed him," Heidi said. It was a statement.

Itzhak nodded. "Yes. Anyway, children," he continued, "the KGB are going to have a lovely open-and-shut case of espionage, sabotage, kidnapping, and death to deal with before many more hours have passed."

He branched off onto a secondary road, along which they headed back in the direction of their hideout in central Moscow.

As they had correctly assumed, Professor Iliya Petrovitch Nevsky was picked up by a passing car a few minutes after the explosion tore through the roof of the van with a thunderous roar, sending fingers of fire into the sky.

Only the professor, standing about a hundred yards up the road beyond the rise, and watching the dense, lingering black smoke rise higher and higher, could appreciate what a blessing in disguise the blaze was.

Nevsky had already considered various ways of disinfecting the wrecked vehicles in the immediate environs after the containers had been blown apart—the dangerous contents scattered but not destroyed by the explosion.

The fire, feeding on gasoline, soon covered hundreds of square feet of road, and constituted the most potent germicide in the world. The flames gave off a veritable roaring sound, as the wind stirred them afresh.

The professor was taken back into town and left at a Militia station. There, Professor Nevsky gave his report concerning the attack and hijacking.

Quick phone checks to the university and his wife fully corroborated that this man was, indeed, who he claimed to be: Professor Iliya Petrovitch Nevsky, member of the Soviet Academy of Sciences and highly respected comrade of the Party.

Half an hour later, he was back at home with Vera, who embraced her husband with relief.

They were once again alone.

He said, "It's over, my dear. And I'm fine. There's nothing more to worry about now."

"But you're trembling, Iliya."

"I can't help it."

"What about our friends?"

"They were all well—all of them. I hope they still are."

"And your driver—was he someone we know?"

"No. I never saw him before in my life. They took him prisoner, but I don't think they'll harm him."

Professor Nevsky was reminded of his active part in disarming the man—obviously a KGB Agent. No doubt, matters would not end here, but for the moment there seemed no point in worrying Vera more. His own head, however, was in a whirl.

The maroon Volga met no obstacles on its return journey to Kurumalinskaya Street. But they had passed fire engines and Militia cars speeding toward the explosion, their sirens screaming.

So far, neither the van driver nor the man from the escort car had spoken a word.

Baruch and Itzhak thought it was time to try some

preliminary interrogation—before they reached their hideout.

First, Baruch addressed the van driver in Russian.

"Give me your name."

"Boris," the man replied solemnly—probably giving the first name that entered his mind.

"Do you want to go home alive?"

"Yes."

"You have a family?"

"Yes."

"You want to see them again?"

"Yes."

"Then you've got to cooperate. Do you understand?"

The Russian did not reply.

"We know you're an old NKVD and KGB member. A man with your occupational hazards is damn lucky if he reaches retirement age. Why die now, instead of enjoying your rights of a senior citizen, together with your children and grandchildren?"

"*Karasho*. What do you want of me?"

"Listen carefully. We are your enemies. We've already killed a dozen of your kind. One more body to be disposed of would not make the slightest difference to us. We'll probably have to bury *him*." Baruch indicated with his head the second prisoner, quite happy to know that he also was hearing the threat. "A grave for two takes little longer to dig than a hole for one. Can you understand?"

"*Karasho*. What do you want me to do?"

"What happened inside the van between you and the other man."

"He hit me! He's one of you!" The Russian cursed.

"I don't know what you're talking about," said Baruch. "Who was he?"

"A fucking professor!" The Russian spat with contempt.

"A professor?" Baruch said, astonished. "What were you doing with a professor?"

"He's in charge of the laboratories. Don't ask me. You probably know more than I do."

"Cut the shit, comrade. Also, we only have *our* orders, and those said nothing about a professor. All we were told was to hold up your van, stop it. Blow it up, if possible."

"Blow it up?" the Russian asked in growing surprise, mingled with the respect of a thug for a fellow professional. "Why? What's in that crate that's so important? Who are you working for, anyway?"

"I'm the one who's asking the questions. So far, I'm doing it politely. You said you want to get out of this alive. Hell, there's only one way you can."

"How?"

"By doing a little job for us. And never mind who we are."

The Russian grinned.

Baruch was left without doubt that "Boris" would promise them anything—as long as they promised to let him go. He was equally convinced that the old KGB hand would be at his headquarters within the hour, breaking his promise to those "traitors," and giving his superiors an exact description of their appearance, as well as a fairly accurate repetition of everything they'd said. He would also report the condition under which he had been released.

"Maybe I'll do it. Maybe."

"I'm intrigued about what you told me about the professor. I suppose he panicked when he saw you draw your gun. I'm sure that's what it was. He must have thought you were one of us. He must have thought you were going to put a bullet in his guts. That makes sense."

"I suppose it does," the Russian agreed, and Baruch was able to discern belief in those words. Later, back at the Cell, *99* would be asked to send a message to Nevsky telling him that he was to follow the same line of explanation, if the Militia or KGB asked him why he had hit the driver.

Baruch continued talking to "Boris." "So I've figured out that the professor has something to hide that we want to know. Here is where you get your one and only chance to stay alive. I want you to set the professor up for a snatch. Do you understand me? . . ."

Baruch had banked on the obtuse process of analytical thinking in the thug's ugly head.

The Russian was momentarily hesitant. It sounded too good—too stupid on his captor's part to be true. Either this was all bluff, some complicated game of cat and mouse, and he was being played with, or they would really believe his promise and let him go. In either case, he had nothing to lose.

"*Karasho,* comrade. I'll do it. I hate those fucking intellectuals, who don't do half the work and get double the pay. One professor less is not going to give me sleepless nights. Let me go. I'll do what you ask."

Baruch quickly explained in English the gist and outcome of his conversation with the Russian.

Itzhak disagreed with his strategy.

In order to confuse their listeners even further, the three now spoke among themselves in Hebrew. Heidi was excited. Nothing could protect the professor against KGB's suspicions better than this "plot" to abduct him, with the help of "Boris."

"We'll take the one, but we kill the other," said Itzhak. "It's got to be."

Baruch said " 'Boris', you mean?"

"Yeah."

Itzhak was already slowing down the car, along a stretch of road where there were deep snowbanks.

He stopped the car and ordered the Russian outside.

"Boris" was obviously frightened for his life. He knew what was going to happen. Itzhak walked him into the snowbank and, without waiting at all, shot him three times. The man dropped dead immediately.

Itzhak covered him as best he could with snow and walked back to the car.

They drove on.

Nobody spoke—their other prisoner, least of all, because he was pale as paper, and shaking in his boots.

Soon, they were coming along the Sadovoyeh Ring. They dared not lose more time in deciding the immediate fate of the other prisoner. Once he was permitted to pinpoint the Cell's Kurumalinskaya hiding place, he could no longer be allowed to go free.

Heidi said, grimly, in Hebrew, "You crooks have just concluded one of history's most dishonest deals." She paused. ". . . If you're going to do what I think you are."

"Main thing is, it'll work," Itzhak said.

"Take my word for it," said Baruch.

Their second prisoner remained silent. He was already scared to death.

Now it was *his* turn.

Baruch went through his pockets. Somehow, all three Israelis had been experiencing a strange, intuitive dislike for the swarthy stranger who had wordlessly looked at his captors with venom in his dark eyes.

The contents of his inside coat pocket held the explanation for his hostile behavior.

In that pocket, they found a diplomatic passport bearing the emblem of Iraq.

A second document, as well as a letter on embassy stationery, showed him to be "Assistant Military Attaché"—a temporary appointment. The letter contained specific instructions authorizing him to accompany the "consignment" from Moscow to Bagdad.

Baruch, whose Arabic was better than Itzhak's, translated the letter for them.

"We should have gone through all the pockets—the truck driver's, that other man's. We just didn't have time," Itzhak said. Then he added, "This *khavaja* will have to be our guest." He spoke grimly.

"You'll pay for this," the Iraqi said. "I know what I know."

"At this moment, *we're* playing the balalaika. And, you shall dance to our tune."

"You might as well let me go now. You can't keep me for long here in Moscow." He was trying to bluff.

"We'll keep you—*if* you behave. If we can't, we'll dispose of you."

The Iraqi's mouth opened wide. His eyes were glazed. "You wouldn't dare!"

"You've seen what happened. Your friends from Black September have dared to do more at Munich,

Athens, and Lod. What makes you think we hold your blood dearer than your Terrorists hold ours?"

The Iraqi did not answer.

Itzhak took the turning in the road that led them along the shortest route remaining—to Kurumalinskaya Street.

He was determined.

. . . 19

They pulled up outside the entrance to No. 99. Heidi reconnoitered to make certain that no one was on the stairway.

Then, handcuffing the Iraqi to himself and with Baruch on the other side, Itzhak walked him up to their apartment, whose door stood open to receive the group without one moment of avoidable delay.

To their surprise, *99* was waiting for them.

He gave them no reason, but they felt fairly certain they had been shadowed by one of the Cell members. It was common operating procedure.

"Here we are," said Itzhak. "And with a none too happy guest."

It took the three Israelis no more than three minutes to give *99* a rundown of what had taken place since two o'clock.

The entire operation had taken no more than two and a half hours.

99 agreed that the first thing to do was to get rid of the Volga parked downstairs. The Cell leader disappeared for an hour and confidently told them, on his return, that the car—for all intents and purposes—had ceased to exist.

The Iraqi's name, according to his passport, was Abu Assad. He was quartered in the "conference room," which faced the back yard and had a single shuttered window.

Both Itzhak and Baruch showed the man pistols, with silencers. There was not the slightest doubt left in his mind, that the Israelis would much rather kill him at once than risk discovery by the Russians.

"Make any noise, break any windows, do any shouting, try to attract any outside attention, and you'll be sorry," said Itzhak.

The Iraqi just stood there, a murderous expression on his face.

During the late evening hours, two other Cell members arrived, and the Iraqi was interrogated by them, in turn, throughout the night.

Accepted Security Branch methods of persuasion were put into effect. These did not include the cruder types of physical torture, but were surprisingly effective nevertheless.

Because at first, all Abu Assad said was, "No! I'll tell you nothing!"

He was cured of his stubborness within an hour.

He denied any knowledge of the containers—and the cholera germs they stored.

But shortly after midnight, he made a full confession, which brought into full light the details of the Liberation Front Fatah Contamination Plan. Had even 10 percent of it succeeded, tens of thousands of people living in Israel—Jews, Moslems, and Christians alike—would have been affected with the disease.

Besides Abu Iyad and George Habbash, the brains behind the fiendish scheme were Wadi Haddad and Ahmed al Yamani, Dr. Habbash's close associates.

The reason for taking the containers to Bagdad instead of Damascus—which was much nearer to PFLP Headquarters—was nothing more than part of the smokescreen being prepared by Habbash and his men to enable them to disassociate themselves from the germ warfare massacre, once it became public knowledge.

The Cell sent an urgent message to Tel-Aviv informing Max Roth, David Boran, and their superiors of the successful completion of this part of the Security Branch commandos' mission—and ending with a request for instructions with regard to the captured Iraqi.

The Moscow morning papers on Monday, December 25, carried no banner headlines about an act of treachery and sabotage by subversive forces or enemy agents.

Both *Pravda* and *Izvestia* gave the affair only a quarter column on an inside page, under the benign heading ANOTHER ACCIDENT ON THE HIGHWAY TO SHEREMETYEVO.

The item briefly described the crash, and referred to the fire as its direct aftermath.

Abu Assad had told them that the other man they had killed was the Military Attaché himself. Eventually, *99*'s contact verified this information, thus strengthening the confidence of the Iraqi's interrogators in the truthfulness of his other statements.

With the Arab held prisoner, the already uncomfortable living conditions at the apartment became oppressive.

On Tuesday, December 26, a message arrived from Tel-Aviv instructing them to check carefully to see if the Iraqi was cosmetically disguised, and to send both full-face and profile photos. Accordingly, the Israelis washed his hair and examined its roots through a powerful magnifying glass under which even an hour's new growth would be detected.

They also checked his eyes for Haptic lenses, and looked carefully for signs of plastic surgery.

"Well, I'm glad that's done," said Itzhak. All the results were negative.

Heidi said, "Things are moving, aren't they?"

"Yeah. Like molasses."

That day, however, a meeting was arranged for Heidi and Vera Nevsky.

The entire Moscow Militia, and a specially reinforced KGB contingent, were scouring the city for two counter-revolutionary saboteurs. It was thus not advisable to endanger Nevsky or themselves by repeating a group meeting like the one held at Kiev railway station on December 20.

Instead, the professor had been asked to let his wife give all the relevant information in answer to the questions received from Tel-Aviv, and prepared by Itzhak.

The obvious reason for choosing Heidi to meet Vera was that—so far as *99* and the other Cell members had been able to learn from their contacts, the Militia and KGB were seeking only two male saboteurs.

Heidi and Vera met in the restaurant of GUM's.

Vera had arrived first. She had chosen a table in the far corner, as distant as possible from the milling crowd of shoppers. She didn't hide her pleasure in seeing Heidi again.

"Hello, my dear. How are you?"

Heidi embraced her and assured Vera that she was well.

Her husband had given Vera an envelope containing the answers to the questions asked by SB Tel-Aviv.

These were briefly as follows:

Professor Nevsky had been personally in charge of preparing the viscous solution which contained living cholera bacilli. It was a highly secret process, the formula and preparation for which was known only to Nevsky and one of his closest associates. No additional quantities had been stock-piled.

The necessary laboratory equipment and raw materials were still in the cellars at Mokhavaya Street, but there was no indication that they would be used in the near future.

The length of time required for producing a quantity sufficient to threaten a modern drinking water system again would be six to eight months.

The professor thought it neither wise nor practical to destroy the laboratory equipment, which could, in any case, be reproduced within three months. Without Nevsky's know-how and research data, no other scientist would be able to operate this equipment—and Nevsky would certainly not lend his skills to such an enterprise a second time.

Heidi read the explanatory papers and put them into her handbag.

"Are you reassured now, my dear?" asked Vera.

"Yes. And thank you very much. Of course the danger will never be entirely removed. But it's certainly been averted for quite a long time to come."

"Yes, I'm sure it has. And if it ever becomes imminent again, Iliya will certainly let you know." Vera hesitated, and frowned. "Please keep in touch with us. We don't mind a little danger, really."

"Thanks, Vera. We will." She paused, watching Vera's face. "How is Iliya? Does he feel safe?"

"Yes. He's fine. I'd know if he were at all worried. He's now working on quite a different project, something to do with virus infections, I think."

"We wish him luck. Please thank him for us."

When the women bade good-bye, Vera pressed Heidi's hand tightly.

Soon after Heidi's return to Kurumalinskaya Street, the coded message containing Professor Nevsky's replies was prepared for dispatch to Tel-Aviv.

The message originating from the Moscow Cell crossed with one coming from Roth and Boran. It informed the three Israeli agents that Abu Assad should be held by them for as long as possible. Serious suspicions concerning his true identity and position in the Arab Terrorist network were being entertained.

For their escape from Russia, the Cell was requested to complete arrangements by Sunday, December 31.

"Time's running damn short," Baruch said.

"Time is always short for us," said Itzhak.

On Thursday, December 28, Max Roth and David Boran prepared the message that was to seal the fate of the temporary Iraqi Assistant Military Attaché in Moscow. They had been working on the task in Roth's office since the early morning. It was now midafternoon.

Roth's fingers drummed on his desk. "Will we ever be done?" he asked.

The information that went into this fatal message had been checked and rechecked a number of times before being confirmed by Roth and Boran. Then it was sent for final confirmation to the highest authority.

At 6:00 p.m. the final draft was ready for approval by the Ministers for Foreign Affairs and Defense, and the Prime Ministers.

"It's done, by God!" Roth said at last.

Thereafter, the message would be coded and

dispatched by an intricate system of radio relays. The secret wavelength would be available only after midnight.

"So there's time for us to read it again," Roth said. "Do it out loud, Dave. I've always been able to concentrate on a text best when I can listen to it with my eyes closed."

"OK, Max. Of course, it may look a bit queer if someone comes barging in through the door. I mean, you with your eyes shut, and everything."

"All right, Dave. Enough humor. Lock the door on the inside and start reading."

David Boran began to read. "Cell Moscow—Commando 'I' Shalom. Case Abu Assad verified and final. Assad is alias. Real name Subkhi Numeiri. Bagdad born. Syria educated. Joined Fedayeen Command 1956. Transferred Al Fatah 1968. Short service ZAIKA Command. Friendship with Wadi Haddad. Brought to personal notice of George Habbash. Recommended for loan to Black September by Ahmed Al-Yamani. Friendship between Yamani and Subkhi very intimate. Yamani requests Habbash that Subkhi return for PFLP special assignment. Black September requests Subkhi participate planning major operation in Germany. Our evidence sufficient proof Subkhi shared base command of Munich massacre September 1972. Yamani repeated request for Subkhi return. Habbash agreed after quarrel with Arafat. Subkhi returned Damascus end September. Immediately attached to Command New PFLP Germ Warfare Division. Spent October inside Israel in charge of water-system espionage. Sent to Russia November. Responsible for germ container shipment. Therefore in category of vicious enemy and convicted murderer. I.E.O. approved by G-M-D R/B."

I.E.O. stood for "Immediate Execution Order."

"Couldn't be clearer," Roth commented, in a matter of fact voice, as if they had just drafted a commercial contract. "A bit long, though."

"Yeah. But I'm afraid to cut any more. I wonder

whether Heidi and the boys will notice that we left out the regulation closing line."

"You mean: 'confirm successful compliance?' " Roth asked. He was smiling grimly.

"That's exactly what I mean, Max."

"Well, we meant that as a vote of absolute confidence in them, didn't we?"

"We did. We sure as hell did. And they deserve it."

"They also deserve to return to our sunny climate and lovely beaches as soon as possible. Good luck to them!"

"Good luck to them, indeed!" Boran repeated. "But tell me, Max. When have you last been above ground? If I remember correctly, before we came down here it was pouring rain, and about eight degrees above zero."

Roth smiled wryly at his companion.

. . . 20

During the five days following their raid, Heidi and Itzhak devoted as much time as possible to improving their knowledge of the Russian language.

Besides the grammar, the recorded lessons, and Baruch's tuition, they made a point of speaking Russian with *99* and the other Cell members.

The message from Tel-Aviv arrived on the evening of Friday, December 29.

One of the Cell members was left in the "conference room" to guard the Iraqi as *99* joined the others in Heidi's and Itzhak's bedroom for a discussion.

When all four had read the message through, Itzhak said, "The implication is to carry this out as quickly as possible."

99 added that preparations for the three Israelis' "evacuation" from Russia were being finalized for Sunday, December 31.

Heidi looked at them and blinked, "Tomorrow is Saturday," she said.

"So?" said *99*.

"Well, I'm not religous. I'm not even Jewish," said Heidi. "But still—I mean, it is your Sabbath."

"What do you think, Baruch?" Itzhak asked.

Prompted by the solemnity of the subject under discussion, they had almost instinctively reverted to the use of their real names.

"Not a practicing Jew myself, as you know, but I guess Heidi has a point. If it has to be tomorrow, fine. But does it?" asked Baruch.

"I don't understand this discussion," said *99*. "Since when does the SB care about Holy Days?"

"It's not a question of caring about religion as such, *99*, but why not keep a little bit of Jewishness in our hearts?" Itzhak said. "After all, it's a Jewish war we're fighting. A little tradition never did any harm. We don't exactly carry the Shield of David into battle like the Crusaders' Cross, but that doesn't mean we have to go out of our way to defy or defile our religous laws."

99 smiled significantly, "OK, I leave it to you, Itzhak, especially since the point has been raised by Heidi." He paused. Then he said, "And since it's already after dark—which makes it Sabbath now—your alternatives for the Iraqi's execution are tomorrow night or early Sunday."

"Are we going to tell him?" Heidi wanted to know.

"I think . . . yes," Itzhak said slowly.

Baruch spoke just as slowly, but more softly, "Please, not more than a few minutes beforehand."

"Who'll do it?" *99* asked. "It has to be one of you."

"Naturally, *99*." Itzhak considered the problem. Everyone waited silently to hear him speak.

"Let it be at dawn on Sunday. Baruch and I will draw lots. Agreed?"

There was unanimous consent.

99 only said: "When you say 'dawn,' you don't actually mean daylight, I think. That would be a bit late, considering all that will still have to be done to get you out of the country the same day. Besides, darkness will make it easier for you to dispose of the body."

"About five a.m.?" asked Itzhak.

"Yes," said 99. "Fine. You'll have to remain Samuel Meiersohn, Paula Ginsberg, and Misha Lipsky. We'll keep it like that, because not a single case of enemy agents smuggling themselves out under the guise of immigrants to Israel has so far been discovered. We would certainly have heard, had there been. In fact, the whole world would have heard! It's exactly the sort of thing the Russians use to help their propaganda. Remember that so-called hijacking attempt in Leningrad?"

"Have they just failed to discover previous cases, or were there none?" asked Itzhak.

"To the best of our knowledge, yours in the first. That sort of thing endangers the entire immigration program, and you know how Golda feels about that. Of course, your operation here has justified all risks, even the one affecting immigration."

99 paused. "Your chances of getting out are good—in spite of the ID problem. What works in your favor is Russian psychology. They make it a practice to think with the minds of their enemies. In this case, they'll say: 'Israel is anxious to do everything to promote more and more immigration from the Soviet Union. Their government will allow nothing to jeopardize our arrangement to grant exit permits to so many thousand Jews per year.' And, in accordance with the Russian way of playing things, they'll be least on the lookout for you checking transports of immigrants."

Itzhak brought the conversation back to the subject of Subkhi Numeiri and his execution.

"You said that we'll have to dispose of his body, *99*. OK. I understand that you can't handle that for us. But can we have your guidance?"

"Naturally." *99* spread a map of Moscow on the table. "There'll be a small commercial van at your disposal. Put the body in the back, and drive out here—beyond Ostankino Park. They're paving a new road there. Work doesn't begin before seven-thirty or eight in the morning, but before the road gang arrives, a mechanical plough clears away the snow from the surface. It's snowing now, and the latest weather report is for continued light snowfall for tomorrow."

99 paused. "Park your car here. Walk to this corner of the botanical garden, which gives you a view of the road-building site. Wait until you see the snowplough drive away. It usually does about six-thirty or seven, which gives you plenty of time to take your car to one of the snow heaps piled up by the plough—a long time before the workmen arrive. Because of the construction work, this is now a dead-end road, and you can expect no traffic.

"As soon as you have buried Numeiri in the snowpile, make a U-turn and come back. There'll be plenty of shovels on the spot left there by the comrades, even though it's against regulations."

Baruch's comment was dry. "Very convenient," he said.

Itzhak said, "OK, *99*. As far as disposal goes, I see no problem. Now, Baruch, let's draw lots. The long matchstick for the man who gets the job. Heidi . . ."

Heidi took two matches from a box, and broke one in half. Then she held them firmly between her thumb and index finger so that only their red sulpher tips showed. "Three draws," she said.

On the first draw, Itzhak got the broken match. The second draw made them equal.

No one spoke.

Tension in the room was high. Experienced secret agents and SB commandos though they were, they had previously only killed in combat—or out of dire necessity. A coldblooded execution was something else.

On the third draw, Baruch again pulled the longer matchstick from between Heidi's fingers. He would have to be the killer.

On Sunday, December 31, the inhabitants of the apartment at No. 99 Kurumalinskaya Street rose at 4:00 a.m.

They made tea, and offered a glass to their prisoner.

The Arab had not been given any reason to suspect that this was his last hour.

Yet the unusual activity in the apartment, the unavoidable tension on the stern faces of his captors, their taciturnity, and, finally, their taking him into the bathroom handcuffed, instilled him with forebodings.

"What are you doing to me?" he asked, again and again.

At last Baruch remained with him alone.

Itzhak took Heidi into the "conference room"—the most distant room from the bathroom.

Baruch closed the door. The Arab sat crouched on the floor in a narrow space between the tub and the basin.

"Your name is Subkhi Numeiri," Baruch began,

and continued uninterruptedly. "You're a member of Black September and the Liberation Front. You helped plan the Munich massacre of our eleven sportsmen. You were caught by us in an attempt to ship germ warfare materials to the Middle East, in preparation for the ruthless and indiscriminate murder of men, women, and children in Israel. You've been tried in your absence in Tel-Aviv, and found guilty on this and other charges, for which there can only be capital punishment. Do you have anything to say before you die?"

Baruch raised his pistol and pointed it at Numeiri's head. The prisoner answered in a low, solemn voice.

"Whatever I say won't stop you from killing me. Allah is great, and Mohammed is His Prophet!"

He closed his eyes and waited for death.

The whispering *pop* of Baruch's pistol could not be heard behind the closed door of the conference room.

Baruch completed the unpleasant task of disposing of the body. He washed the blood from the tub and bathroom floor and he carried the body down the stairs.

He pushed the dead Arab into the deep snowpile near the botanical garden, as planned.

As he carried the body across the snow, he felt as though everyone were watching him.

Another one was dead.

Itzhak had offered to help him carry the heavy, lifeless body down to the car, but Baruch had declined.

"No. Let me finish it. Maybe you'll want to touch Heidi's body tonight. You'll both be glad that you can do it with hands that didn't carry a human carcass."

"Thanks, *haver,*" Itzhak used the word for "friend," so commonplace in Israel, so loaded with meaning here and now in faraway Moscow.

99 arrived at eight o'clock in the morning.

He looked inquiringly at the three Israelis, and read the answer to his unspoken question in their eyes. He sighed with relief. They drank Nescafe and ate an unusually substantial breakfast.

Perhaps it was the knowledge that this would probably be their last day together that made the atmosphere more formal than usual.

99 began his briefing over the breakfast table.

Let me fill you in on some details you ought to know. According to the rules and regulations that go with immigration from Russia to Israel, your donors handed in their passports on the thirteenth, when they received the *rasresheniyas* I brought you the next day. They also got permits for purchasing foreign currency. With these they bought a hundred and twenty dollars each at their bank a few days ago. I am going to give you this money now, together with the confirmation of sale issued by the bank." He handed each of them a large brown envelope containing the money and printed form.

"Keep these handy, together with your exit *rasresheniya,* when you get to the airport. Next, your donors had to bring the heavy luggage to the airport bus terminal in town five days ago. Here's a list of their luggage and its contents. Try to memorize this in the few hours you have, before leaving for Sheremetyevo. Here's the terminal receipt form on which it is stated that the suitcases have been checked by customs and weighed in. You won't see them until you arrive in Vienna."

99 continued: "You'll be surprised to note how generous the Soviets are with their weight allowances. There are practically no restrictions for expatriates leaving the country for good—just one of those unpredictable inconsistencies of bureaucracy. As for hand luggage, the taxi which is coming to pick you up—driven by one of us, naturally—will bring the permitted number of pieces. This will be more thoroughly searched at the airport, and so will your clothing and shoes. There may also be a more intimate body inspection, but that's rarer nowadays. At this point, you'd better hand me your weapons, or anything else that could cause trouble."

The three Israelis went to their rooms and piled all such items on the table. Pistols, first-aid kits, flashlights, a compass, passkey, combination pen-knife—anything which an ordinary Russian-Jew was unlikely to carry with him on his way to immigrate. They went through all their pockets, not forgetting their overcoats.

"What kind of questions are we likely to be asked by the border control?" asked Heidi.

"Normally, almost none," said *99*. "They're very taciturn. In fact, anything more than the usual: Are you so and so? What is your age? Address? Birthplace? Name of parents? Questions more probing than these would be a warning sign that they suspect something. Of course, you'll be asked whether you're taking out any unauthorized valuables. And you aren't," he added, smiling.

Baruch asked, "Could there be any questions regarding family left behind in Russia?"

"It's unlikely. But bone up on your ID descriptions. Any more questions?"

There weren't.

"Here are your Aeroflot tickets to Vienna. They cost a hundred and twenty rubles, each, paid for with our Israeli taxpayers' hard-earned money."

"And very generous of them," Itzhak said, with a grin.

"You're flying by Tupolev—TU one thirty-four, a very comfortable, medium-sized plane. They say the food is excellent. Your scheduled flying time to Vienna is one hour and fifty minutes. I hope you enjoy your flight."

"You should have become an airline steward," said Heidi.

99 had made it sound so simple—as if the Militia and KGB were not on the lookout for three supposed East German scientists, whom a certain Professor Staniev had revealed to be frauds, still missing and not aprehended. As if two unidentified male saboteurs had not blown up a valuable secret cargo only seven days ago—men who must now be desperate to get out of Russia.

99 must have been thinking the same thoughts because he said: "We don't believe you three should arrive at the airport together. On the other hand, we couldn't very well organize three taxis to be driven by our Cell members. So we're taking you from here to the Kiev railway station. There, Heidi gets off with her things and takes a cab to the airport. At the White Russia railway station, Itzhak takes a taxi to the Aeroflot terminal, and gets on an airport bus. Baruch remains in our taxi, which will take him to the terminal."

"How should we act when we meet?" asked Baruch.

"Act as though you're acquainted, but not very close friends. That will be more natural than pretending you've never met before. Jews applying for immigration to Israel sometimes wait years for their day of exodus. They're likely to have run into each other on a few occasions, and to be pleased to meet at Sheremmetyevo. There'll certainly be several other immigrants on your flight to Vienna, and you'll be able to observe them and their reactions as they meet."

"There's just one more thing to talk about," said Itzhak. "And, that is—what have you planned for us after we get to Vienna?"

"From here on in, you're under the kind safekeeping of Max Roth and David Boran. Obviously, you'll join the flock of immigrants at the Vienna airport, and listen to a welcoming speech by the representative of the Jewish agency who is always there to meet newcomers. And from there, you go to the Schoenau Transit Camp, like all the others. After that, I have no doubt you'll soon be picked up and whisked away by one of our SB friends."

After a short silence, Heidi said what was in all their minds.

"I wish we were that far already!"

. . . 21

Informed that customs and border patrol procedures could take from one to three hours, the Israelis left Kurumalinskaya Street in a taxi driven by one of the Cell members, at 1:00 p.m.

Heidi got off at Kiev station without a wave of good-bye. Baruch and Itzhak—now, once more, Misha Lipsky and Samuel Meiersohn—took separate routes but met again at the Aeroflot terminal, as they were getting on the airport bus. They exchanged polite greetings, but sat in separate seats.

Heidi got to the airport ten minutes earlier than her two fellow agents.

They joined the line of passengers separately, waiting to have their hand luggage and clothing searched.

Heidi and Itzhak were separated by five persons, Itzhak last, with Baruch farther ahead. They had decided that it would be best to have him through customs and K.P.P. first—and close enough to help them as unobtrusively as possible if they got into difficulties with their Russian.

This, of course, remained their major handicap.

In spite of feverish efforts their vocabularies were still not adequate to cope with unforeseen situations. Their main emphasis had been put on eliminating any overt traces of a foreign accent from those few phrases which they had learned to speak.

The line moved slowly. But their turn at hand baggage inspection finally came.

The official merely glanced at their tickets and nodded to a plainclothes Militia officer, who went through their belongings with minute care.

He opened tubes of toothpaste, and prodded the contents of Heidi's face cream. He felt the sides of their travel bags for secret compartments.

"Would you please remove your shoes now?"

He was speaking to Itzhak.

Itzhak did so.

The official picked them up, and bent the soles so sharply that one of them broke at the instep.

"I'm very sorry about this, I assure you."

Those were the last words he spoke to them. He waved them on in the direction of the K.P.P. border control desks.

With satisfaction, they realized that they were not being sent to one of the cubicles on the left, inside which Militia men and women in uniform were conducting body inspections.

"So far, so good," Heidi said to herself. Obviously, they had not aroused suspicion yet, but they knew the time had not come to heave sighs of relief. The line leading to K.P.P. was even longer than the one in front of customs—a sure sign that each prospective passenger was undergoing the most painstaking scrutiny.

It was almost four o'clock when Baruch—purposely retaining his position in line, and well ahead of Heidi and Itzhak—at last faced the KGB officers conducting the check.

One took his papers and handed the currency purchase form and its ticket to a second officer.

He kept the *rasresheniya,* spread out on the desk in front of him.

"Misha Lipsky?" he asked as he looked up, after minutes of studious silence spent comparing the face, height, and weight of the person standing before him with the photo and verbal description on the permit.

"Da," Baruch said.

The official asked him all the expected questions: origin, age, education, place of residence, place of last employment, family status. It checked out perfectly. The other official handed Baruch his ticket and currency voucher.

"What other valuables have you? Gold? Precious stones? Art objects?"

"Nothing, comrade."

"All right. You may proceed, Lipsky." He tore off the lower half of the *rasresheniya* and put it into a metal container.

He gave the upper section back to Baruch, and turned his attention to the next person in line.

"One Jew and Russian less. And good riddance!" he muttered under his breath.

Baruch divined this without undue concern. He was conscious of the official's "Lipsky" in reply to his "comrade."

Heidi received the identical scrutiny and was asked the same questions. Then Itzhak. Neither of them experienced difficulty in understanding or replying to the standard questions. Their voices carried not a trace of foreign accent. They had learned their lessons well.

But they knew it was not over yet.

By 4:20 p.m., the formalities were completed. In a way, it was little different from the procedures at Lod and other international airports.

In Israel, no passenger could get through without at least a perfunctory body search. Here, paradoxically, they had been spared this indignity. At London airport, there was visible electronic and X-ray equipment. Here there was none.

Without speaking to one another, merely exchanging friendly nods, they glanced at their watches. If their TU 134 to Vienna was not delayed, they should be called for embarkation in about ten minutes.

A staircase led up from the K.P.P. station to the lounge, from which passengers proceeded to the departure gates. On their way up, travelers were afforded a last opportunity of waving farewell to freinds and relatives.

A Militia man stood at the bottom of these stairs to prevent close contact between the departing traveler and those remaining behind. A KGB agent also kept a careful eye on all those mounting the stairs.

Normally, it was not a very strategic spot.

Smugglers—of whom there was no dearth at Sheremetyevo—had usually been caught before reaching this stairway. Spies and traitors getting this far would be safe from here on to the plane, unless some last-minute order from KGB Headquarters arrived in time for an interception.

Today, the KGB man mused. Another lot of Jews off to the Holy Land. He watched them going up the stairs. He mumbled under his breath, recalling a propaganda broadcast on Moscow radio the night before: "And, I wonder how many of those Jews will want to come back to Mother Russia, before a year has passed!"

One by one, as they ascended the steps, they turned to wave—sometimes to relatives, often to well-wishers who had come to see them off on their journey. The KGB man was paying no special attention.

Then Baruch went up without turning to wave good-bye.

A dozen persons later, Heidi ascended. No last farewells.

Itzhak followed. He didn't turn once for a last glimpse of wife, children, uncle, niece, neighbor, or friend.

Unusual!

The KGB man decided to give these friendless and solitary immigrants some highly trained and undivided attention.

Mounting the stairs unhurriedly, he followed the three Israelis into the departure lounge.

The best undercover agents often slip up because of the most trifling mistakes . . .

Had the three Israelis been aware of the KGB agent's suspicious eyes upon them, they would first have carefully examined their own actions for errors.

It would be only fair to say that *99*, in planning their escape, had overlooked the matter of relatives and friends. So had Itzhak, Baruch, and Heidi. So had the other Cell members.

Even the brilliant Roth and Boran would most likely have failed to pay due attention to this aspect of airport custom.

The three Israeli agents' decision to keep apart, and not display any obvious signs of friendship, helped keep the KGB agent in a state of uncertainty. Of course, he had the authority to pick these people up for questioning, but—a typical Russian official—he loathed the thought of possibly making himself ridiculous in the eyes of his superiors. And, after all, what did he have to go on? What was his reason for suspecting three of these Jewish immigrants?

Suddenly, he remembered.

Three East Germans had recently disappeared from the Hotel Berlin. They had not been caught either escaping across the border or inside Russia. What had been their crime? He could not recall.

Neither was he certain whether they had been men, or two men and one woman. Nor their ages and descriptions.

A phone booth near the top of the stairs drew his eye. He decided to check these details before taking more drastic action. He entered the booth, keeping the three suspects in view as he dialed.

It took him four minutes to come up with the information he needed.

Two minutes before he had finished in the phone booth, the Vienna flight was called and the passengers, including the Israelis, had begun to file out through Gate 11.

The gate was out of sight of his booth.

The choices open to him, therefore, were breaking off his call to headquarters, or having his suspects exit through the gate before he got the information he needed.

But the plane would not leave at once, and the KGB agent felt confident he would still have time to have them brought back—or take them off personally—once his suspicions were confirmed.

Baruch, Heidi, and Itzhak did not plan to make overt contact prior to their arrival in Vienna.

They handed their boarding cards to the hostess at the gate, and went down the gangway to a bus waiting to take them to the plane.

Only a few short steps to safety!

Meanwhile, the KGB agent received the information he'd been waiting for: two men and a woman whose descriptions fitted his three suspects closely enough to warrant their apprehension. If he was mistaken, there was still enough time to put them on the next plane to Vienna, due to take off about eight hours later.

He quickly left the phone booth, and walked over to Gate 11.

That was his first serious error.

Had he instead phoned the control tower, and instructed them to signal the plane, the fate of the Israelis would almost certainly have been sealed at once. But his direct pursuit through Gate 11 was not subtle enough to escape the attention of a nearby man wearing an inconspicuous Aeroflot uniform . . .

99 had been very open and frank with his friends, the three Israeli agents, most of the time.

In his experience as a Cell commander inside, potentially, the most dangerous capitol in the world, he had to do things his own way, without always waiting for detailed instructions from Tel-Aviv. He was often obliged to make decisions and take risks far beyond those planned "at the green table" back home.

Moreover, he was not only an undercover agent, a sensitive part of the ruthlessly efficient SB network, he had also grown to like his three guests at Kurumalinskaya Street well over and above the call of duty.

Their welfare and safety had been made his concern. And purposely stretching his responsibility to the limit, he was determined to insure their safe departure from Sheremetyevo Airport.

Wherever they had gone thus far, one of the Cell members had been assigned to shadow their movements—and the movements of anyone trying to trail them. *99*, however, had decided to take this particular watchdog job—their last hours on Russian soil—into his own hands. The Cell had a stock of Soviet uniforms—Army, Navy, Air Force, Militia, and, of course, Aeroflot.

99 had no difficulty entering the departure lounge upstairs on the footsteps of the KGB agent, whom he had at once recognized as one of the "regulars" at Sheremetyevo.

The KGB agent's unusual ascent of the stairs immediately in the wake of the three Israelis had at once activated the well-tuned antennae of *99*. He had watched the agent's movements upstairs, and his sudden entry into the telephone booth.

When Heidi, Itzhak, and Baruch had gone out through the exit gate, *99* had, for a moment, hoped his instincts were deceiving him and that his intervention would not be necessary.

But two minutes later, when he had observed the agent rush out through the gate, *99* knew what he must do.

Reaching the open gate, which gave him a straight line of vision down the gangway and out onto the tarmac of the field, he saw to his relief that the bus carrying his friends had already departed for the plane. The KGB agent, with obviously nervous impatience, was waiting for the next bus, which would take the final group of people out to the waiting Tupolev.

99 knew he had very little time to act.

Walking brazenly past the ground hostess at the gate, he strode down the gangway, jostling the passengers in his way, and answering their grumbles rudely.

The moment he reached his man, he addressed him in faultless Russian, which in the KGB agent's experience placed him way up in the "intelligentsia" class.

99 took the agent confidently by his elbow and said:

"Please. Come with me. It's a matter of great urgency."

"But I, too, am engaged on an urgent mission," the agent said.

"I know," said *99*. "We're after the same people. I can't identify myself here."

"How do you know who I'm after?"

"I got an urgent message one minute ago. Please!

People are listening. *You* know we must not be overheard!"

99's emphasis on "you" did the trick. This could only mean that the uniformed Aeroflot officer was in touch with KGB. How else could he have recognized a colleague?

The man said, "But I myself only spoke with my superior five minutes ago." Then he lowered his voice, putting his lips near *99*'s ear, and continued, "And we must not allow this Vienna flight to take off before I get on it—and do what I must do."

"Naturally, comrade," *99* whispered in return. "Come. We shall go to the control tower and tell them to hold the plane until we get there."

This assurance removed the agent's last doubts. He followed *99* up the gangway and back into the departure lounge.

A hostess rushed toward them. She was angry. "You shouldn't race through here like that, comrade."

"Keep quiet and don't interfere!" the KGB agent told her. "Those female busybodys!" he said, when they were out of earshot. "Women in uniform are only good as officers' whores." He winked at *99*, who smiled warmly in agreement.

They were making their way through a door marked: AIRPORT PERSONNEL ONLY—PASSENGERS KEEP OUT!

They entered a narrow, empty corrider at the far end of which was a stairway leading up.

Neither *99* nor the agent had ever been to the control tower.

"We must search the plane," said *99*. "Take off all the passengers. These are terrorists who have accomplices aboard. They may try to hijack the aircraft."

"Incredible! And here, at Sheremetyevo!" The KGB man was excited. What a blow to airport security. His own reputation was at stake.

They had reached the foot of the narrow staircase leading up.

To his right, *99* noticed a door marked: MEN'S ROOM.

There was no one else near. *99* allowed the agent to

advance a step ahead of him. Then he pulled out the pistol in his shoulder holster. The safety catch was off. The bullet entered the agent's head, traveling upward from his neck, spattering bone fragments, blood, and brain, onto the opposite wall.

99 caught the sagging body before it fell to the floor, and pulled it toward the men's room door.

But the door was locked.

. . . 22

The three Israelis showed the numbered coupon of their boarding cards to the hostess aboard the plane, and were politely shown to their seats. The interior of the Tupelov 134 was small enough to enable them to see one another easily.

Only about two hours more, Heidi thought blissfully, and our "separation" will be over. She was hungry for her husband and a full-size bed.

Baruch closed his eyes and relaxed, as soon as they were told to fasten their seat belts. He tried to shut out the memory of a crouching form, wedged in between the bathtub and basin—and the way it had dissolved into a shapeless heap when he pulled the trigger. He had no regrets, and felt confident that, once asleep, he would dream about better things: sunny beaches, lovely girls in bikinis, and long cool draughts of beer.

Itzhak thought about Iliya Petrovitch Nevsky. What a fine man! Did he represent a majority of Soviet scientists and intellectuals? As a Sabra, Itzhak had grown up in a society largely founded and perpetuated by Jews originating in Russia, but he had never quite accepted this pioneering down-to-earth Russian Jewry as true representatives of their complex Nation. Indeed, he had often argued, had they been able to fit in, so many hundreds of thousands of them would not have run for their lives, or deserted to North and South America, Palestine, and a score of other countries.

To put it all down as a result of the 1917 revolution, and Bolshevism, was quite an invalid line of reasoning.

After all, Jewish intellectuals had been the pioneers of Marxism, and red socialism, in the Western world.

Moreover, the mass of the Soviet people had accepted and identified with the new leadership and socialist system in their homelands throughout the Union. Violent dissent was the exception, rather than the rule.

While these thoughts passed through Itzhak's mind, the plane had taxied to the runway in readiness for takeoff.

Belatedly, he, too, fastened his seat belt.

The plane's powerful jet engines screamed in anticipation of flight. Rushing into the icy wind, it rose above Sheremetyevo, Leningrad Highway, Gorki Prospekt, the Kremlin, and Red Square—flying west.

The three Israeli agents on the plane were blithely unaware of the plight in which *99*, who had probably saved their lives, found himself back in the airport building.

When he found the men's room door locked, *99* did the only thing left. He let the dead man's body lie where he had shot him, at the bottom of the stairs.

99 had begun his business with a grand bluff. He hoped his luck would hold if he tried to end it in kind. He mounted the stairway, which proved to be longer than he expected. It went up straight for fifteen yards, and then made a ninety-degree turn to the left. There it ascended another ten yards before leading to another long corridor, similar to the one below.

99 made his decision to go up just in time. He had barely left the last step behind him when two uniformed Aeroflot stewardesses came out of a door marked WOMEN'S ROOM, and squeezed past him on their way downstairs. They turned their faces toward him only briefly.

He pushed open the door of the ladies' room with his foot—ready to offer profuse apologies—and found it empty. Closing the door behind him, he walked to the farthest of the four separate cubicles, went in, and bolted the cubicle door. A second later, he heard the loud shouts of shock and fear from whoever had found the dead body.

There were more shouts, arguments, and commands.

Several pairs of feet ran past the toilet. There was an increasing number of male voices.

99 waited thirty minutes, until the hall outside was silent. Then he left the cubicle. Going to the door leading into the hall, he pushed it open slightly. The hallway was empty.

He could hear a number of voices one floor down, though now they sounded hushed and controled.

He descended the first flight of stairs and glanced around the corner, confident that the risk involved was small. The focal point of the group down there lay on the floor, bleeding. It was not likely that someone should be keeping an eye on the steps.

What *99* saw more than justified his audacity.

Among the people below were three officers in Aeroflot uniforms. Why should they notice a fourth?

His only critical problem remained his descent. He decided to make it straightforward.

He hurried down the stairs, not stopping until he reached the lower floor.

The body was being removed. The wall and floor were already being cleaned.

A uniformed group which appeared to be the crew of an Aeroflot plane went past him on their way upstairs. They stepped on the spot where the dead KGB agent had lain less than an hour earlier.

99 strode into the departure lounge and mingled with the crowd.

At the bottom of the stairway, a new KGB agent had already replaced the dead comrade. As *99* passed him, he nodded.

"If I stay in Moscow much longer, they'll probably make me an honorable member of the KGB," *99* reflected silently, a grim smile on his thin lips.

Once outside the airport building, he leisurely walked to the parking lot, got into his car, and drove away.

His friends would be anxiously awaiting his return.

As his car entered Gorki Prospekt, *99* was already thinking about the wording of his message to Tel-Aviv, which would go out tonight.

"One Arab Terrorist leader and one KGB agent expedited," he mused, adding with rare grandiloquence: "All in a day's work."

Mission accomplished.

On Sunday, January 6, a summing-up meeting was held in Max Roth's office at Security Branch headquarters in Tel-Aviv.

Today's meeting was something in the nature of a final tidying-up and evaluation session which, in Israeli military parlance, is termed: *Lekakhim.*

The three Israelis had not spent more than twenty-four hours at the Vienna airport before being taken to the Vienna Cell. There they received their Israel passports, and El-Al tickets—as well as a bottle of Champagne, with a congratulatory note from Max Roth.

When they had reported back in Tel-Aviv, Roth had been away, but Boran had welcomed them warmly. He gave them the news of *99*'s bravery at the Moscow airport, telling it in his best raconteur style, so they experienced surprise, guilt, and shock, followed by admiration, gratitude, and relief.

"The grand bluff more often than not succeeds," said Boran.

"Yes," Roth agreed. "If it's combined with a cool head—and absence of childish pride."

"How do you mean that?" Dr. Slonin asked.

"Quite literally, my dear Slonin. Imagine what might have happened to *99* had he disdainfully declined the shelter of a ladies' room."

Heidi said "I might add a tale or two about living conditions at the Cell on Kurumalinskaya Street. Not much room for pride there either—especially a woman's."

"I'll recommend a two weeks' paid holiday at the Hotel National, corner Gorki and Marx Prospekt . . . after diplomatic relations with the Soviet Union have been reestablished, of course," said the member of Parliament.

"So long as it isn't the Hotel Berlin," Baruch said, with a laugh. "We still owe the bill there."

"Let's get down to serious business," said Boran. They all agreed. "I'll read an account of this operation, and then I propose a brainstorming session. It's all over now, with the main danger behind us. So we can speak freely and in retrospect."

He took out three sheets of paper from his pocket and began to read.

He read for a long time—about the complete operation in Moscow, with comments, questions, and praises for *99*. He ended, "Our Moscow Cell would probably have been blown wide open had *99* fallen into KGB hands—a development with far-reaching political implications about which I know we shall hear more from our M.P."

The discussion which followed lasted five hours.

In spite of the friendly atmosphere that prevailed throughout, there was as much difference of opinion expressed as consensus. On one point alone was no dissenting view put forward; a great tragedy had been averted by their outstanding success.

They all agreed that no aim can justify every means, but, as Dr. Slonin put it in somewhat unimaginative university English, "You can't bake the cake without breaking the eggs."

When their official discussion was over, and the tapes were handed to a girl in Army uniform with Intelligence insignia and lieutenant's bars on her epaulettes, Roth turned to Luke and Dov, who were also present, and said:

"I've heard you guys are disappointed that we didn't call on *you*."

"We sure are, sir." Luke spoke for the two. "After all—we've been a team so often."

"And a successful team, too. Dave," he said, "I think we'd better do something to cheer these guys up." He winked at Boran. "Give them those envelopes, and let's send them home to study."

Colonel David Boran had come prepared. He took two large brown envelopes from his briefcase, and handed one each to Luke and Dov.

The envelopes bore the offical seal, and were marked "Top Secret."

Dov frowned, "Just the two of us?" he asked.

"We'll see. Baruch deserves a bit of rest. Heidi and Itzhak probably need a few quiet days in bed. And when they've all recuperated, don't worry. I've got three more envelopes waiting in my desk."

ABOUT THE AUTHOR

Born in Austria in 1926, HARRY ARVAY began his involvement with underground operations in 1938 as a youthful member of the "Free Austrian Movement." He escaped to England in 1939; by 1944 he was working with British Intelligence, interrogating German POWs. After the war, he was engaged in undercover work against underground terrorist organizations in India, Japan and China. Arvay moved to Israel in 1950. Soon after his arrival, he was on the trail of Fedayin raiders near the former Jordan-Israeli border. Arvay now lives and works in Tel Aviv. His suspense novels include: *Eleven Bullets for Mohammed, Operation Kuwait, The Piraeus Plot* and *The Moscow Intercept.*